ALL I NEED

RACHEL HANNA

FOREWORD

All January Cove books can be read in ANY order, so feel free to pick up any of the books in this series at any time.

I would also like to offer a FREE January Cove book to you as well! Just click on the image below to download your copy of WAITING FOR YOU.

CHAPTER 1

*B*rad Parker was anything but serious, but this morning he was feeling very serious. His bank account was dwindling a little more than he'd like, but such was the life of a contractor, he supposed.

Still, being a single guy running a crew of contractors didn't leave a lot of time for a life, especially a love life. For the last year, he'd watched all three of his brothers, and now his sister, fall in love with their soul mates. It was like something was in the water, and he was avoiding the water.

Right now, the focus had to be off women and on money or he was going to be living in a homeless shelter. Of course, he was being dramatic as he knew his mother, Adele, would never let that happen.

She'd have him a room set up in the Parker house in a heartbeat, but he didn't want that. He was a grown man, and he needed to support himself accordingly.

Always the funny one in the family, Brad had been finding it increasingly difficult to smile lately. It had been a few weeks since his brother Kyle married his love, Jenna. Just before that, his sister Addison gave birth to beautiful Anna Grace, and she was cozily cuddled up with his long-time friend, Clay Hampton, now.

And then there were Aaron and Tessa, and Jackson and Rebecca too. Even his mother was making strides to move on with her life after rekindling an old friendship with Harrison Gibbs. And then there was Brad. Funny. Outgoing. Never bothered by anything.

Yet he was bothered. Very bothered. Agitated even.

His personality felt like it was changing from fun-loving to jealous of his siblings and even his mother. He felt left behind like some kid who'd lost his mother at the grocery store.

Sure, he dated every now and again, but nothing ever lasted. Either the women didn't get his sense of humor or they were flat out boring. And boring women made him want to poke his eyes out. He'd had one real love relationship, but he didn't like to talk about it. He didn't like to talk about what she'd done to him.

Right now, he was more worried about money than women. He'd lost the Davenport job, a major contracting opportunity, in downtown January Cove. His bid had come in lower than the competition, but that didn't matter when the competition was related to someone on the board of the corporation buying the plaza Brad had bid on.

He'd been counting on that job, and when it didn't come through he found himself floundering around, analyzing everything about his life.

He sat at Jolt, staring at his phone. The banking app he used had to be wrong. It was early summer now, and that monetary figure should've been higher. A lot higher.

"Hey bro," Kyle said as he walked into the small coffee shop and slapped Brad on the back. He wasn't really in the mood for it this morning.

"Hey."

"Wow. That's the least I've ever heard you speak. You okay?"

"Not in the mood, Kyle," Brad said. So far, he'd been able to keep his personal issues private, but it wouldn't be long before his brothers would figure it out. When he stopped talking and cutting up, something was majorly wrong.

"Chill, man. Things can't be all bad," Kyle said, waving his hand at Rebecca to bring his regular. Coffee. Black.

"I guess not. You live in a lovesick, puppy dog, permanent honeymoon world. The rest of us don't," Brad mumbled, and even he was starting to hate himself.

"You need a date or something?" Kyle asked, smiling wryly until he saw that Brad was serious. And that wasn't right at all. "Okay, what's wrong?"

"Nothing," Brad said, sorry he'd opened his big mouth. Rebecca put Kyle's coffee on the table and smiled before walking back to the register to wait on a new customer.

"You can't fool me, man. Either 'fess up or I'll tell Mom."

"Seriously? You'll tell Mom? What are we, twelve?" Brad said, finally cracking a smile.

"I can totally revert back to twelve anytime," Kyle said before taking a sip of his coffee.

"Fine. Business just isn't where it needs to be right now." Brad couldn't even make eye contact with his brother. It was embarrassing. The Parker men worked hard, always had. It was the one thing they all had in common. Well, that and good hair.

A man was supposed to support himself, take care of his family. How would he ever have a family if he couldn't take care of himself?

"Contracting is hard. I know, trust me."

"Yeah, but you have steady work. You buy a fore-closure, fix it up, sell it. I have to bid on jobs, and there just aren't many jobs in January Cove lately. I've been considering..."

"What? Leaving?" Kyle asked.

"Yeah. Maybe. I don't want to but..."

"You can't leave. It would crush Mom."

"Kyle, I can't live my life for everyone else. I've got to do what needs to be done."

"I agree, but I came here to deliver some good news to you, and it looks like I was just in time," Kyle said, a smile spreading across his face.

"Is Jenna pregnant?" Brad asked, immediately jumping back into his nosy personality.

"No. Not that kind of news," Kyle laughed. "But we practice nightly," he remarked with a wink.

"Gross. So what's this wonderful news? You won the lottery?"

"I wish, but no. Actually, it's about you."

"Me?"

5

"Yep. My pal, Jordan Gates, called me last night. He said the Drake Corporation bought the Lamont Theater."

"Lamont Theater? Man, we had some memories there, didn't we?" Brad said smiling as he traveled back in time in his mind to the old movie theater across town where they'd kissed a lot of girls and sneaked into a lot of R rated movies.

"Oh yes we did. Remember their popcorn?"

"Man, it literally melted in your mouth. And their arcade was my home away from home," Brad said, smiling at the memories of the only time in his life where responsibilities seemed a million miles away.

"Yeah. I think I still have high score on that Pac-Man machine..."

"Pac-Man? Okay, you're showing your age."

"Shut up. Do you want to hear the news or not?" Kyle said, taking another sip of his now chilled coffee.

"Yeah, but what does any of this have to do with me?"

"The job is yours if you want it." Kyle grinned and waited for Brad to let the words sink in.

"Wait. What?"

"Jordan's uncle is on the board at Drake. The company is based in California. Anyway, they needed a local contractor who had good ties to the community because they want to do some big tourist stuff here. The Lamont is just the beginning apparently."

"Tourist stuff in January Cove? Not sure how that'll go over around here."

"Well, the Lamont has been closed for at least five years now. The economy could use a boost, plus it would open jobs. Gotta sell the bigger picture to the old timers."

"Um, Mom would be included in the old-timers, you know," Brad said.

"We'll deal with her later," Kyle said chuckling at the thought of his stubborn mother. "Anyway, the job would be overseeing the whole thing. You'd have to hire a crew and work with their manager who's flying in from California as we speak. And here's what your income would be..." Kyle said, sliding a piece of paper across the table. Brad's eyes almost bugged out of his head.

"Seriously? That's what they want to pay me?"

"Yep. Not too shabby, brother. I might need to borrow some money soon," Kyle joked. "The manager will meet with you tomorrow on site. They're sending the contract paperwork for you to sign, so you'll need to handle that when you meet at eight sharp in the morning. The manager's name is on the paper too. Some guy named Ronnie."

Brad sat stunned across from his brother, shocked at how quickly life could change. He'd been lamenting his life all morning, honestly considering a career change, and then a miracle had happened.

"I don't even know what to say," Brad said with a grin pasted on his face. He hadn't felt this hopeful in weeks, and now a weight felt as if it'd been lifted from his shoulders.

"Well, first you can say what a fantastic specimen of a man I am, and then you can get that goofy grin off your face before someone sees you," Kyle said as he stood and smacked his brother on the shoulder. "I'm always here for you. You know that, right?"

"I know that," Brad assured him as he stood to meet his brother's gaze.

"You'll find her," Kyle said with a knowing smile on his face.

"Who?"

"Her. The one for you. She's out there, Brad. You've just got to find her."

"What makes you think I want a woman in my life right now?" Brad said, trying to play off the fact that his brother was totally right. They walked outside onto the sidewalk, the warmth of the summer sun beating down on Brad's neck.

"Because I know you've got to feel unsettled with all these couples around you now." How did his brothers always know everything? It was irritating.

"Whatever. I'm too busy right now, and life's about to get even busier apparently. Thanks for everything, Kyle. Really. You saved me this time."

"Always do... Have a good day..." Kyle called back as he headed down the sidewalk to his truck. Brad looked down at the paper in his hand, and felt his stomach churn as he looked at the number again.

He couldn't screw this opportunity up.

It was 7:50AM, and Brad had been sitting in the parking lot of the Lamont Theater for almost twenty minutes trying to psyche himself up to go inside. Normally self assured, this was new ground for him to actually be nervous. He'd always been the Parker kid who made everyone laugh, always creating havoc wherever he went with pranks and jokes that made his mother cringe.

But today he couldn't summon any courage at all. This was big money. This was a big corporation. His entire career was on the line, and he had to make a good impression on the manager flying in from California. If he didn't like Brad, there was a good chance the job would be given to someone else.

So today his idea was to behave. Simple as that. Behave like a grown up. And for some reason, Brad felt completely nervous about that. He was much more comfortable setting up whoopee cushions for his brothers or making farting noises in front of his sister than he was right now.

He looked down at the paper Kyle had given him one more time. The manager's name was Ronnie Blair, so Brad committed it to memory so as not to mess up the introduction. He'd practiced it in the mirror a few times that morning just to see if he "looked professional".

He stepped out of his pick-up truck and walked toward the front doors of the Lamont, a place he'd come to many times during his formative years. His family saw Sunday matinees there a lot, but mostly what he remembered was making out with Becky Sue Polland in the ninth grade. She had the softest lips, but she later turned out to be a girl's field hockey coach… and then decided she played for the other team, so to speak.

The thought made Brad laugh a little, but he

reined himself back in quickly as the front door opened before he could touch it.

Standing in front of him was a woman unlike he'd ever seen in his life. She was petite, but it felt like she towered over him. Her presence was felt before any words left her mouth. Her blond hair was slicked back into a tight ponytail, and her blue eyes stared at him as if he was a bug that needed to be squashed.

"Uh… hi…" Brad stammered. Nice start, idiot.

"Good morning. Can I help you with something?" she asked, pointedly, as she looked around him as if something better might come along any second. It kind of irritated Brad.

"I'm here to meet Ronnie. He'll be expecting me." He squared his shoulders, holding his briefcase next to him… although it was empty minus one manila folder and a notepad inside. He was trying to look professional.

"Oh, he will? And you are?"

"Brad Parker. I'm the contractor hired to oversee this project." Again, he stood up straight and looked directly into her eyes, letting her know that he was in charge.

"Please, come in," she said, opening the door. He followed behind her, trying in vain not to stare at her body as they walked to the front desk of what used to be the movie theater. He'd bought hundreds of movie tickets there, but all he could look at right now was her tight butt in a very fitted business suit. Damn. He really needed a date. Immediately.

Maybe he would add that to his notepad. Task number one - get a date.

She quickly turned before his eyes had a chance to return to their sockets, but her expression was not one of thankfulness for the compliment of him staring at her butt. No, it was the look of a potential axe murderer who was not at all pleased he'd been staring at any part of her. Maybe she also coached girl's field hockey.

Brad cleared his throat, nervously trying to find the nearest exit sign. What was it about this woman that was making him have hot flashes like he was a menopausal female?

"Mr. Parker, can you tell me exactly what your background is in commercial contracting?" she asked, crossing her arms and pursing those gorgeously full lips of hers. Wait, who was she to ask him about his background?

"With all due respect, ma'am, I think I'd rather talk with Ronnie about my qualifications. I'm not accustomed to chatting with the assistant or secretary about my background." She snorted lightly out of her nose, and he saw the first hint of a smile. Only it wasn't a "Hey there, how are you?" kind of smile. It was more of a "Hey, jackass, why don't you go play in traffic?" kind of smile.

"So you don't talk to the 'help' is what you're saying, Mr. Parker?" she said as she leaned her hips against the bar where he'd ordered thousands of sodas over the years. He wondered for a moment what she'd do if he hoisted her up on that bar and... "Mr. Parker?" she repeated.

He reached up and checked his own lips for possible drool before he responded. "I never said 'the help'," he muttered. She was beautiful, but she was also the most irritating woman he'd ever met.

"Look, I don't really have time for this right now. I've got a job to do, so if you can just point me to Mr. Blair, I'd greatly appreciate it."

"Miss Blair."

"Excuse me?"

"You're looking for Miss Blair."

"No... I'm looking for Ronnie. Are you here just to be difficult?" he asked, crossing his arms and showing more irritation that he would have expected so early on a Monday morning.

"Ronni Blair," she said, reaching out to shake his hand. "That's Ronni without the 'e', by the way."

Brad stared at her, as if her words made no sense to him. He wasn't the sharpest knife in the drawer, but right now he felt downright stupid. "You're the manager? From California?" he stammered.

"Ah, there you go. Finally figured it out, Einstein," she said with a wry smile as she pulled her hand back before he ever shook it. She crossed her arms again. "And I again ask what kind of experience you have as a commercial contractor? Or do I not deserve an answer because I'm a woman?"

She was impossible! "Being a woman had nothing to do with…"

"Didn't it?" she interrupted.

"Look, your board hired me…"

"And they gave me the final say so, Mr. Parker. So far, I'm not seeing what they did."

His stomach lurched, and he worried the sausage biscuit he'd eaten that morning was coming right back up. Yeah, that would be quite impressive to her. Breakfast in reverse on her fancy stiletto heels… that were attached to her perfectly contoured legs….

"Mr. Parker?" she said, waving her hand in front of his face. "Are you prone to daydreaming like this all the time? Because that can be quite dangerous on a job site like this."

"I'm not daydreaming. And yes, I do have plenty of commercial contracting experience. The bank you drove past this morning on the corner of Main and Sunset? That was my project, start to finish. And the library renovation was my baby too, so I can assure you that I have the necessary qualifications." Now he was just talking on autopilot out of sheer determination. He needed this job badly, and even the sexiest woman on the planet wasn't going to derail him.

"Nice to know, however I think that I need to interview a few other candidates before making a final selection." She turned and started shuffling some papers on the bar, and he felt like lunging and putting his hands around her perfect, swan-like neck. Only he would never put his hands on a woman in anger, and he probably wouldn't strangle that neck anyway. It would be better to put a hickey there like he'd done to Tanya Cantrell back in tenth grade.

"You can't do this project without me," he said with conviction. She slowly turned.

"Pardon?"

"First of all, you're in the South now. Don't be all

fancy in the way you talk. We're kind of laid back around here."

"Thanks for the advice," she said, rolling her eyes and smirking.

"Secondly, you need my help to get this job done. The community around here isn't going to immediately embrace a project like this. In fact, they'll probably fight it, and you need me to help you overcome that."

"Mr. Parker, you do have a rather high opinion of yourself. However, we have the proper zoning already in place to do everything we want to do here. The community doesn't have to agree to anything." She held her head high, jutting her chin forward.

"Oh really? And just who do you think will pay to enter your establishment once it's built?"

"Tourists."

"I hate to break it to ya, but tourism in January Cove is just starting to grow. No way in hell it's going to pay the bills. You need the locals to make this whole thing work, and without a Parker or other prominent community member, you might as well go ahead and hang up the out of business sign now," he said, hoping like heck that she believed what he was saying. It really was true, but she didn't seem to believe much he'd said so far.

She stared at him for a moment, her piercing eyes making his skin shiver a bit, even in the warmth of the closed theater. She licked her top lip, and it took everything he had not to hide his bottom half behind the counter. Being attracted to a snobby woman wasn't his plan for the day. First on the agenda would be to get a date with someone, and fast. He was obviously overdue for a little female attention.

"Fine, Mr. Parker. We'll approach this on a trial basis."

"No trial. Either I'm your man, or I'm not," he said, regretting the choice of words immediately. She smiled, and it almost looked genuine.

"I hope you'll bring this level of determination to the job," she said, holding out her hand to shake his. "Welcome aboard."

He grasped her hand. It was soft and warm, probably like the rest of her body. He pulled his briefcase around to the front of his jeans to hide the growing excitement he was trying to knock back down. Sometimes being a man sucked. Women could easily hide their attraction to someone, but not men. When they were attracted, it was like having a jack-in-the-box in their pants.

"Now, if you'll come with me, I'd like to sit down and discuss the project..." she said, oblivious to the new placement of his briefcase. He followed her, being careful to keep his eyes up.

CHAPTER 2

*A*aron sat on his front porch, staring out over the campground that he called home. His business was flourishing now that summer was in full swing. January Cove was teeming with tourists, and many of them were renting spaces in his RV park and cabins that were scattered throughout the property.

Aaron and Tessa had originally planned to turn a nearby property into a bed and breakfast, but had put those plans on hold until Tessa and Tyler could get settled into January Cove. In reality, Aaron wasn't sure he wanted to add running a B&B to his list of responsibilities, but he could see living in that property one day with his own family.

"Hello, handsome," he heard Tessa say as she walked up behind him and hugged his neck.

"Well, hello there..." he said, tilting his head up and meeting her lips with his. They'd had a romantic evening after Jackson and Rebecca had offered to keep little Tyler for the night. Aaron and Tessa had definitely needed the time together. Tyler was a rambunctious three year old, and they didn't get a lot of time alone.

"You planning on working today?" she asked as she walked around him and eased herself down into his lap.

"That depends..." he said, his lips against hers again.

"Depends on what?"

"On how late we can get Jackson to keep..." he started to say as he saw his brother's truck pulling into the campground. They both sighed simultaneously.

"Mommy!" Tyler yelled, way too loud for the early morning hour, as he ran to Tessa. She stood at the edge of the stairs now, ready to embrace her son like the perfect mother she was. Aaron was still lamenting his bad luck that he wouldn't get more time alone with her.

"Bro, what the..." Aaron started to say as he

looked at Jackson with exasperation. "I thought you were keeping Tyler busy for a few more hours…"

"Sorry, man. I got a call on the Cambridge deal in Atlanta. Whole thing's falling to pieces so I have to drive up there and woo a couple of clients. I texted you an hour ago, but I guess you were busy." Jackson said with a wink. "Rebecca's at Jolt…"

"I understand. No biggie," Aaron said shaking his brother's hand. "Thanks for keeping him last night. I'm sure he had fun."

"I'm sure you guys had fun too," Jackson said with another wink. Tessa waved and thanked Jackson before ushering her son into the cabin they shared with Aaron.

"Yeah. It's never enough time. Having a little one is exhausting," Aaron laughed.

"I wouldn't know… but I hope to one day soon."

"Oh really? You thinking of popping the question soon?" Aaron asked.

Jackson leaned against the log railing and smiled. "Maybe. She's the one, for sure. Just gotta figure out the logistics of it all. I still own my place in Atlanta and my place here, so there's that to deal with. And the business."

"Well, I'm sure you guys will work it out. She's been good for you," Aaron said.

"You think so? She's a great woman. I lucked out. And you did too," Jackson said, cocking his head toward the cabin. "When are you going to make this official?"

"I don't know," Aaron said, a hint of a smile playing across his lips.

"Don't wait too long, brother. Women worth marrying don't sit around waiting for long," Jackson said as he walked down the stairs and toward his truck.

"So I've heard…" Aaron called back with a laugh before Jackson drove away.

As Brad sat across the table from the world's most beautiful woman, he thought about his bad luck. Why couldn't the manager have been an ugly, over-weight, wart-covered man with bad breath and an even worse toupee?

Oh no… She had to be supermodel gorgeous with a brain that overpowered her amazing good looks. She had to smell like heaven mixed with coffee mixed with sex.

In an effort to appear professional, he tried to keep his eyes down and focused on the paperwork they were going over at the table. The arcade had been transformed into a makeshift office space while the renovations were going on. Gone was his favorite Pac-Man machine, replaced instead by a small table with a fax machine and landline phone.

"Mr. Parker? Did you hear me?" she asked, cocking her head to the side as she sighed. His ADD seemed to be in full swing around her.

"Sorry. Could you repeat that?" he said without looking up.

"Is something wrong with you, Mr. Parker?" she asked. Damn, even her voice was sexy.

He looked up, gazing into her deep blue eyes. They were like perfect reflections of the ocean down the street. Swirling, sometimes stormy, with glints of light.

"Please, call me Brad."

"Okay, fine. Brad, is something wrong?"

"This place just holds a lot of memories. I came here all the time growing up."

"Tell me about it," she said, shocking him to the core. She wanted to hear his memories? Not at all what he expected.

"Well," he said, standing up and starting to walk around the place. "This is where my beloved Pac-Man game was. And no matter what my brother says, I still hold the high score. And over here was where the snack machine was. We bought Milk Duds and M&M's from here..."

"We?"

"My three brothers and I. I have a sister too, but mainly it was us boys that came here a lot."

"Go on..." she said, standing and following him as he walked.

They walked out into the lobby. "This is where we bought soft drinks and popcorn. The machine was right here, and the cash register was right here. I remember that because Tiffany Ames worked the cash register and she was very popular with the guys..." he stopped himself, realizing that he was getting a little too personal. He could've sworn he heard her giggle a bit under her breath. "Anyway, down here is Theater B, which is where most of the movies were shown. The G rated movies were almost always in Theater A."

They walked into Theater B, and he was shocked to see that the seats were still there. It looked just like it did when he was a teenager, only the place now smelled of stale popcorn and cigarette smoke.

"Wow..." he whispered as he stood there, looking down the aisle toward the screen. She was behind him, only a few steps, and he could feel her presence.

"Lots of memories?" she asked softly.

"Yeah," he said as he turned and looked at her. Were they having a moment? Her whole demeanor - her tone, her eyes - had changed.

"I bet you had a lot of dates here, huh?" she asked, a small smile playing across her face.

"I did," he said, grinning like a school boy.

"Lots of kissing, 'necking', as they used to say?"

"We never said necking. It wasn't the fifties," he chuckled.

"Brad?" she said softly as she looked him square in the eye.

Maybe she felt it too, that spark between them. Still, they'd only known each other a couple of hours, so it was a little soon to make his move.

"Yeah?" he said back, taking a half a step closer and looking down into her beautiful eyes.

"Can you get focused now?" The cool tone had returned to her voice, and her face showed no emotion. What the hell?

"Excuse me?"

She backed up a couple of steps, crossed her arms and pursed her lips. "Look, I'm trying to work with you here on a professional basis, but you're not making it easy. You're reliving your youth in this place while I'm trying to work on a multi-million dollar deal. I don't have the time or inclination to take another trip down memory lane with you, so I thought maybe this little tour would get it out of your system for good. Are we clear?"

Rage seethed inside of the normally calm and fun-loving Brad. Never had he wanted to fist fight with a woman so badly. He assumed he was asking too much to hope that she was a black belt in karate so he'd have a reason to fight with her. Of course, she seemed mean enough to kick his ass, so he thought he'd better leave well enough alone.

And the sad part was that she was right. So far, he'd spent the last two hours thinking about his teenage years and fawning over her good looks. He was wasting the opportunity, and he wasn't going to do it again.

"You're absolutely right. I've been distracted." He wanted to add he was distracted by her ass and eyes, but thought that to be inappropriate and would certainly result in her slugging him.

"Good. Glad we're on the same page. Now, I'd like to get back to those numbers, if you don't mind," she said, turning on her stiletto heel and walking toward the door. And his eyes, having a mind of their own, returned to her round butt as it made its way across the lobby.

"Dear God, help me," he whispered under his breath.

"JUST A LITTLE TO THE LEFT. No, honey, the left!" Addison called from the street as her boyfriend, Clay, tried to hang the 4th of July decorations on the front of their bed & breakfast. Their first guests would be arriving any day now, and she wanted it to be perfect for them to watch the fireworks from the front porch.

"Sweetie, I think it looks fine," he called back as he stood a few feet from the porch, looking up at his handiwork.

"I don't want it to look fine. I want it to look perfect," she called back, smiling down at her new baby daughter who was nestled snugly in her arms.

Clay turned and grinned at his girlfriend. She was the perfect woman for him. Her figure had already started to return, and he was having a hard time keeping his hands off of her. Of course, she had been cleared by the doctor to be intimate again a few weeks ago, but having a newborn baby in the house was proving to make romance quite difficult.

But he loved Anna Grace more than he could've

ever imagined. The fact that she wasn't biologically his had no bearing at all on his feelings for her. She was the center of his world lately, a fact that surprised him. Although he'd always wanted a family, he never thought he'd be raising another man's baby.

When he looked at Anna Grace, he saw her mother, but that was it. Of course, he had no idea what her biological father looked like, but he was going to be the best father she could ever imagine. He chose her, and he would always let her know that his love knew no bounds. She was his daughter.

"Hey, sis," Brad said as he approached on the sidewalk.

"Brad, good to see you," she said, leaning in and kissing her brother on the cheek.

"Hey, Anna Grace," Brad said, smiling as he touched her cheek with his index finger. "She's getting so big."

"I know. It seems like everyday she's doing something new. I want to capture every moment of it."

"And she tries, believe me," Clay said as he walked down to greet Brad. "She keeps filling up the storage on her phone with videos and pictures."

Addison smiled. "Well, she's very loved and cuter than any baby I've ever seen."

"And you're not a little partial?" Clay asked, putting his arm around her.

"Nope. Totally objective," she responded. "So what's new, bro?"

"Well, I just started a brand new job today. Total renovation of the Lamont Theater."

"Seriously? Wow, that place holds a lot of memories," Clay said with a grin. Brad was suddenly transported back to the uncomfortable situation he found himself in that morning.

"Yeah. I tried reliving a few today."

"Tried?" Addison asked.

"The manager they sent in from California to work with me... Well, let's just say she's not the cuddliest person. Kind of a tiger. Or a shark. Or some other mean animal. Anyway, she wasn't excited to hear about my memories."

"Hm, sounds like there might be some friction there. How hot is she?" Addison asked. She knew her brother well.

"Excuse me?"

"Oh, come on. California girl with attitude. How hot is she?" she asked again. Brad looked at her and then at Clay before he cracked a smile.

"So hot that my eyelashes were starting to melt."

Addison and Clay cackled with laughter. "That's pretty damn hot," Clay said.

"Yeah, but her icy cool personality quickly saved me. She's a…"

"A what, dear brother? A bitch?" Addison whispered, putting her free hand over Anna Grace's ear.

"I didn't say that…"

"Why is it when a woman is a hard nosed business professional, we are called an ugly name?"

"It's not about that, Addy. She has no feelings, no soul. She's just mean."

"Maybe she's had to learn to be that way to survive in business."

"No, it's more than that…" he started to say, but he noticed that Clay and Addison's attention was elsewhere. A car pulled up beside them, and Brad lost his breath.

Clay and Addison stared at the woman getting out of the car. She was stunning with light blond hair pulled tightly behind her head. Brad let out a low groan, and the pair immediately realized who she was.

"Hi. I'm Ronni Blair. I have a reservation to stay here for the next few weeks," she said, reaching her hand out and shaking Addison's free hand. She was smiling and engaging. Nothing like she'd been at the theater. Brad stood there with his mouth hanging open slightly, wondering how on Earth she could change her personality so quickly.

"Hello again, Ronni," he said as he leaned into her view. Was she purposely trying to ignore the fact that he was standing there too?

"Brad," she said simply and turned toward her car to get her bags. Clay ran down the walkway and helped her.

"Let me show you to your room," Clay said. She followed him up the walkway with Brad's eyes trailing her. When he turned back to Addison, she was grinning from ear to ear.

"What?"

"You've got it bad. I've never seen you so smitten!" she said in a loud whisper.

"Smitten? Really?"

"You're blushing, Brad Parker!" she said with a giggle.

"Addy, shut up."

"What are you going to do?"

"I'm going to do nothing. She's an awful woman, trust me. She's hot, I'll give her that, but she's about as prickly as a porcupine. I'm not getting involved in that nightmare."

"Okay, you keep telling yourself that…" she said,

humming as she walked away toward the house. Brad watched his sister walk inside, but what he was really watching was the image of the beautiful blond standing in the entryway. She was going to be a problem for him. He just knew it.

CHAPTER 3

he next morning, Brad arrived early on the job site. He and Ronni had spent their first day crunching numbers and getting on the same page as far as the job went. Today, they'd be walking the property and making some design decisions so that he could hire the proper contractors to begin the work.

After an evening of watching TV and drinking a few beers, he'd gotten a good night's sleep and was determined to keep it professional today. No staring or drooling or random crotch Jack-In-The-Box problems.

Today was going to be about proving himself as a professional. After all, he wasn't trying to get a date with this woman. She was his co-worker, like it or not, and he would have to deal with her for a few weeks.

He walked into the lobby of the theater and saw her, up on a ladder, measuring a doorway. She didn't see him at first, so he had time to look at her yet again. He shouldn't have, but it was impossible. She was gorgeous, especially when she wasn't scowling at him.

She was wearing a pair of form fitting jeans and a tight gray t-shirt. Her boots were sitting on the ground next to the ladder, probably because they had heels too. This time they weren't stiletto, but they certainly weren't meant for climbing ladders. He put his briefcase, getting fuller by the day, on the counter. It slipped and fell with a thud to the floor. This caused Ronni to swing her head around, and she lost her balance, starting the long tumble to the floor below.

Brad ran the few feet when he saw her starting to fall, and she fell instead into his strong arms, her face coming to rest just inches from his own. She was panting for air, obviously terrified, and he was relieved that she hadn't gotten hurt.

"Are you okay?" he asked, genuinely concerned. He was trying to ignore the fact that she was in his arms, and it felt completely and totally right. His hand was on her butt, and that too felt pretty dang good.

"I'm fine," she finally said, her breath jagged. "Put me down. Please," she said, her face changing to its normal icy appearance. It was a shame, really, because she was so beautiful. The scowling looks she gave ruined a perfectly good thing.

He gingerly put her down until she was standing on her own two feet.

"Glad I was here to catch you," he said, assuming she'd want to finally say thank you for his chivalrous act. Of course not.

"I should be glad? Really? If you hadn't dropped your seventies-looking briefcase, I wouldn't have been startled in the first place," she said, turning to pick up her boots. "Shall we get started?"

"Okay, that was my late father's briefcase, first of all. And second of all, why do you have to be so rude all the time?"

"Sorry about your father," she said softly before continuing. "And second, I'm not rude. I get to the point. That's all."

"Around here we call that rude," he said, picking up his briefcase and walking toward the office. She followed and slipped on her boots once she sat down.

"Well, maybe that's a Southern thing," she commented with a bit of a snicker. He didn't like it one bit. As if Southern equaled stupid or something bad.

"From where I sit, Southern things are pretty damn good, Ronni. And if you're going to do business around here, you'd better learn the way of life."

"I won't be here long."

"Well, I assume your boss wants this to be a success?" he asked, leaning back in his chair with his arms crossed.

"Of course."

"Then maybe you should tone down your attitude and ease up a little. We're at the beach, for goodness sakes."

"I live at the beach in California."

"Not the same thing. People around here are laid back, courteous and expect good manners. They're family people for the most part. They say please and thank you and yes ma'am..."

"No one needs to call me ma'am. I'll scratch their eyes out," she said firmly, but then her mouth formed a genuine smile.

"Wow. Is that a smile I just saw?" Brad prodded. She tried to put her straight face back on, but it didn't work.

"Maybe. See? I'm not all bad."

"I don't think you're bad at all," he lied, although his opinion was shifting moment by moment.

"No?"

"You just need a little Southern renovation yourself," he said. "Come on, let me show you around town."

"We have work to do," she said, reaching for her files.

"Ronni, you need to know the area. The people. The culture of this place. That's part of this whole project. The work here can wait."

She studied his face for a moment and finally relented. "Okay, fine. One hour. But then we come back here and get to the real work. Deal?"

"Deal."

They walked outside into the blazing Georgia sun. It was early July, and the heat was almost overwhelming. Thankfully, they were at the beach, so cooling down was steps away in most cases.

"Listen, you're going to be miserable in that outfit," Brad said, pointing at her jeans and high boots.

"But this is what I brought," she said, looking down at her clothes.

"Really? If you live at the beach at home, why would you dress like that?"

"Well, for one thing, I don't hang out at the beach a lot," she said as they walked toward his truck.

"Why?"

"Because I'm busy. I have things to do."

"And relaxing isn't one of them?"

"No."

"Then why live at the beach in the first place?" he asked, getting more curious about her by the minute.

"Because that's where the successful people live."

"I see. And you're successful?" he asked, opening the door to his truck for her. She stood there staring at it for a moment and then looked at him.

"You're not serious? We can go in my rental car," she said, pointing at the small silver sports car sitting across the lot.

"Um, I'm a pretty big guy. No way I'm folding myself in half to get in that thing." She sighed and stepped into the truck as he held the door open, trying desperately not to stare at her butt as she climbed inside.

Brad got into the other side and cranked the truck up. He noticed her fanning herself already and smiled. "Let's run over to Pellman's."

"What's that?"

"A small department store down the road near the Walmart," he said as he started pulling out of the lot.

"Walmart?" she said, cringing so much that he could see it out of the corner of his eye.

"No, I said Pellman's. They have perfectly nice, beach related clothing for the successful woman on-the-go," he said, smiling at her again. This time, she smiled back slightly, which was progress in his mind.

"I'll be fine in this. Really," she insisted.

"You're going to die of heat stroke, and then I'm going to have to give you mouth to mouth to revive you…"

"Fine! Goodness, you're persistent…" she muttered.

"It's a great quality in a contractor, don't ya think?" She rolled her eyes and didn't answer, instead opting to look out the window at the passing scenery. "So, are you from California originally?" he asked, trying to pass the uncomfortable time.

"You don't have to do the whole small talk thing, Brad. I'm fine with the silence," she said without looking at him. For a moment, it angered him but then he saw something. Pain. Her face was a mixture of pain and sadness, and he didn't know why. Worst of all, he didn't know why he cared anyway. She was just some woman he was working with for a few weeks, and then she'd be gone back to her California life. She was right. Why make small talk?

They rode the five minutes over to Pellman's, and she ran inside. Within ten minutes, she was back outside wearing a sexy little red sundress and silver sandals. She was even more stunning now. Just great.

She climbed inside of the truck before Brad could get out and open the door, which was probably a good thing since he would've had a view of her climbing up. That might have been too much for his poor heart to take.

"Okay, where to?" she asked as she closed the door.

"Well, I thought I'd just give you a little tour of the town. Hopefully it will give you a taste of the people, who they are, where they hang out…"

"Let's get to it then," she said sharply. He started to drive, and avoided looking at her as much as he could.

"How'd you like Pellman's?" he finally had to ask.

"It wasn't so bad," she said, shooting him a small smile.

"Apparently," he said, nodding his head to the bag she had placed at her feet. It was filled to the brim with new clothing, and he was a little excited to see it all in the coming days.

They drove down the main street in January Cove, and he pointed out the major places that the locals frequented. The dry cleaners, the grocery store, the library.

"And that's Jolt," he said with a smile. "My brother's girlfriend, Rebecca, runs the place. She just moved here with her teenage son a few months ago."

"From where?"

"New York. Her husband was killed in the September eleventh attacks."

He heard a small gasp escape from her lips. "Oh no. How terrible. Was he in one of the buildings?"

"Yes. Her son was just a baby really. He doesn't remember his Dad at all, but he and Jackson are getting closer all the time."

"That's good. A kid needs stable parents. I know that all too well..." And there it was. Just a comment, but one that came from her soul. One that showed, finally, that she was human like anyone else.

"I lost my Dad when I was pretty young, so I know how important that is too," he said, as they pulled in front of Jolt and stopped. "Want some coffee?"

"No thanks. Not right now. I'd rather keep the

tour moving along," she said, not making eye contact.

"Okay, but we're going to need to get lunch at some point."

"I brought my lunch."

"And what did you bring?"

"Salad," she said, as if there was no other possibility.

"You really are a California girl," he said with a laugh.

"And just what is that supposed to mean?"

"Salad? Why don't you eat something heartier like a hamburger?"

"Because it will clog your arteries and take years off your life. Not to mention make you fat," she said furrowing her eyebrows.

"But it tastes good, and you only live once."

She shook her head and laughed as they started to drive again. He took her down to the ferry and parked.

"Um, what are we doing?"

"I want to show you something." She looked almost scared. "Don't worry, I'm not going to molest you or anything."

"Do you have any filter on that mouth of yours?"

"Nope," he answered simply before opening his

door. Again, she jumped down before he could get around to help her like the Southern gentleman he was.

"Hey…" Clay called out from the ferry.

"Clay, so good to see you again. I didn't know you ran the ferry," she said, her whole demeanor changing. She was smiling and shook his hand. What on Earth was the problem with this woman?

"I'm surprised your tour guide here didn't tell you," he said, grinning at Brad.

"Didn't get a chance to. We were having such enthralling conversations in the truck." She rolled her eyes yet again and crossed her arms. "Come on."

She followed the men to the ferry, and then allowed Clay to help her up onto the boat. "Where are we going?"

"To the island," Brad answered, pointing for her to sit at the back of the boat.

"There's an island?"

"Yep. Most people don't know about it, except the long-time locals. My brother had his wedding reception there a few weeks back."

"And why do I need to see it, Brad?"

"Because you need to know the whole area, Ronni." He put extra emphasis on saying her name

43

because she had done that to his. It was like the worst game of one-upping he'd ever been a part of.

"I don't see how this…" she argued.

"Jeez, woman, can't you just relax for once? Take a moment to breathe in the salty sea air and enjoy the moment." He was becoming frustrated with the wall she had erected around herself. She seemed nice and friendly to everyone else but him. Had he harmed her in a past life or something?

"Fine. I'll relax," she said in an almost pouting tone. He wondered if she was married or engaged or dating someone, but he dare not ask. She'd probably push him right over the edge of the ferry. But still, he wanted to know if there was a man somewhere willing to put up with her attitude. Right now, she truly had no redeeming qualities as a person except for her beauty, and that made him sad to think. Beauty would only carry her so far in life.

She leaned into the metal railing and rested her chin on the top of her hand as she stared out into the water. And then she closed her eyes, and he could see her taking in deep breaths as if it was a struggle to relax. She was really trying, and the fact that it was difficult was painful for him to watch. Really, why did he care? He'd only just met her, and she'd be gone in a few weeks anyway.

But he did care.

A few minutes later, they pulled into the dock at the island and got off. Clay stayed aboard the boat and pulled off a few minutes later.

"Hey, where's he going?" she asked, almost frantic.

"He'll be back in about twenty minutes or so. He makes runs back and forth all day."

"But what if no one's there wanting a ride?"

"Then he just comes back."

"That seems like a waste of time and fuel…"

"Ronni, relax. This is how January Cove operates." She stood on the dock, still wearing her sandals, and looked at him for a moment before averting her eyes. There was something in that look that he couldn't put his finger on, so he let it go. "Take off your shoes."

"What?"

"You don't want to ruin your new shoes, do you?" he asked. He slipped his shoes off as well before they stepped off the dock and onto the warm sand.

"Come on," he said, urging her into the edge of the treeline in the middle of the island.

"Where are we going, Brad?" He just waved for her to come, and she followed without saying anything else.

"I want to show you my private area," he said without thinking about his choice of words.

"Excuse me?" she squealed, stopping dead in her tracks and holding up her hands like she was about to be attacked.

"Poor choice of words," he said as he turned around and saw her standing a good ten feet away from him. "I meant that I wanted to show you where I spend my time when I come here. I'll keep my private area to myself unless you request a viewing."

Shockingly, she started laughing. Actual laughter. Not a smile, not a smirk, not a giggle. A laugh. It was so beautiful to see her face and hear her laugh that he almost hugged her, as if she'd accomplished something big, like winning a Pulitzer Prize. Instead, he started laughing too.

"You're a strange person, Brad Parker," she finally said after she caught her breath.

"Thank you. And also thank you for laughing at the idea of seeing my private area. Really boosted my self-confidence. Come on," he said, reaching out for her hand to pull her up the dune of sand he was on.

"I've got it," she said, reverting back to her independence as she struggled her way up the sand.

"Suit yourself."

When they got to the top, he led her about ten

more feet to a misshapen tree. One of the limbs hung rather low in an L-shape over the sand. Still, it was a bit of a climb to get up there.

"I'll have to help you at this point," he said, reaching out to take her hand. She shook her head.

"I'm not climbing up there in a dress!"

"Don't worry. I won't look," he said, hoping he could keep that promise.

"Absolutely not!"

"Oh, I see. You're scared of heights?"

"I'm not scared of anything."

"It sure doesn't seem that way."

"Honestly, you're the most infuriating person I've ever met!" she said, finally taking his hand and walking toward the tree.

"Same to you," he said with a laugh as he hoisted her upwards until she could pull herself onto the limb. His hand was squarely on her butt, and he turned his head as he'd promised, but dang how he wanted to look. Or squeeze.

He followed her up into the tree and sat beside her, the bark of tree scraping against the fabric of his shorts.

"What are we doing in a tree, Brad?" she asked, exhaustion apparent in her voice. "I mean, seriously, will you do anything to get out of working?"

"Look," he said, leaning closer to her and pointing off in the distance.

"Oh, hey, there's the bed and breakfast. And Jolt..." she said, naming off all the places she'd seen already that morning.

"January Cove is a small town, with everything compacted close together. I thought coming here would give you a better view of the town."

"I see. So you weren't just trying to get me alone in a tree to show me your private area?" she said, smiling at him. Finally, she seemed like a normal woman with a personality. He smiled back.

"Again, I'm open for viewing anytime."

"That's such a man thing to say," she said, rolling her eyes.

"Oh, come on. I'm sure your boyfriend has to have a sense of humor too," he said, wishing he'd just kept his mouth shut for once.

She cleared her throat and stared off into the distance, not really looking at anything in particular.

"Sorry. Did I say something wrong?"

"No. But maybe we can keep the comments professional?" she said softly. "I don't really want to talk about my private life with someone I barely know."

Unable to shut his mouth off, he continued.

"Well, okay, but has it occurred to you that no one can get to know you when you're so... defensive?"

"Defensive? Look, Brad, I appreciate the tour and everything, but can we just head back? I have a lot to get done today, and frankly, so do you," she said as she suddenly jumped down off the tree without warning. She must have thought the sand below was soft and flat, but instead it was a hill rolling down to the beach below. And it was peppered with small rocks and shells all the way down. Brad had never even tried to jump down that way, but today he did. He followed her down, narrowly avoiding a collision with a rock.

"Ronni!" he yelled, trying to let her know he was coming. She was in a heap at the bottom of the dune, her leg scraped up from the rough landing. He was surprised she didn't break anything with the height of the fall. When he finally got to her, she was in tears, her beautiful face stained with a mixture of water and sand.

"It hurts!" she yelled, pointing at her right leg. He gingerly took her leg and put it in his lap, blowing the sand off of the cut area.

"God, Ronni, I'm so sorry. I didn't know you were going to jump that way..."

"It was my fault. Everything is always my fault…" she murmured through her tears.

"Ronni, what's going on? Why are you running away like this?" he asked softly, much more worried about her mind than her body for once. She looked at him, big crocodile tears still escaping her eyes. "How can I help you?"

There was tension between them as she stared into his eyes, her breathing slowing down as if she was about to kiss him or something. It was confusing and thrilling all at the same time. The jagged edges of her breath caused his heart to pound against his ribcage. Their faces were no more than a few inches apart when Clay's ferry horn started blaring in the background.

"You guys ready?" he called from the other side of the trees.

"Let me help you, Ronni," Brad said softly. She nodded and he carefully picked her up into his strong arms. "I've got you, okay?" She nodded again, and he carried her back to the ferry.

CHAPTER 4

"*I* think you're going to be just fine, Ronni," Clay said just after they'd pulled into port. Luckily, Clay had some EMT training, a necessity for him to be carrying people around on a ferry. It wasn't the first time someone had gotten hurt climbing those misshapen trees or gotten stung by a jellyfish. He kept an ample supply of first aid supplies on the boat.

"Thanks. I appreciate your kindness," she said, her face still stained from tears and sand still caked on her legs.

"Ronni, I'm so sorry," Brad said, for the tenth time since they boarded the ferry. Clay tied the vessel up as Brad and Ronni stood to start walking back to his truck.

"No, it's my fault. I shouldn't have jumped suddenly like that," she said as they walked slowly to the parking lot. She leaned against the side of his truck as he located the keys in his pocket. "I'm not good with personal conversations, Brad."

"Yeah, I believe that now," he said with a half hearted smile. "From now on, I'll keep it professional. Okay?"

"Okay. And thanks... for the view of January Cove. It did help me."

"You saw it for like ten seconds," he said as he opened her door. "Hardly enough time to really understand it."

She climbed into the truck, and he went back around to the other side. He cranked it up, and they headed back toward the theater.

"Actually, it gave me some marketing ideas for when we finally open. For instance, we could partner with some local businesses to give them discount coupons for tourists."

"Good idea," he said, "but first we have to convince the community that this attraction is going to be a good thing."

They rode mostly in silence for the next few minutes. When they parked at the Lamont, she got out before he could open the door. In fact, by the time he was out of the truck, she was inside the building, injured leg and all.

ADDISON LOVED nothing more than staring at her baby girl. Anna Grace was the most beautiful human being she'd ever seen. She had the prettiest, albeit toothless, grin, and the tiny wisp of hair on top of her head barely held the little pink bow Addison had put on it today.

"Hello, my two beautiful ladies," Clay said as he entered the kitchen and wrapped his arms around Addison's waist. She was standing in the kitchen cooking dinner with Anna Grace in one hand and a big spoon in the other. Clay deftly took the baby from Addison's arms.

"Hey, don't steal my baby!" Addison playfully chided as she pushed up onto her tip toes and gave him a kiss on the cheek. But it was too late. Clay was already enamored with his new baby daughter.

"So what's for dinner tonight?" he asked. Now that they were real bed and breakfast owners, Addison was responsible for feeding them and their only guest, Ronni Blair.

"Grilled chicken with a Greek marinade, roasted

cabbage and wild rice with a ginger spiced seasoning."

"Wow, that sounds great," they heard Ronni say from the doorway of the kitchen. Ronni was a nice lady, but very different from most people in town. She was fairly quiet, kept to herself and seemed to be harboring some emotions that were just on the edge at all times.

Addison couldn't figure out if it was just because she was from California, and that was so different from her own Southern roots. Or, did she have some big secret that was eating her up inside?

One thing Addy knew for sure was that her brother had it bad. He wanted Ronni already, but it was killing him because he didn't WANT to want her.

"Oh, hey, Ronni. Dinner should be ready in about half an hour. Why don't you have a seat and keep me company?" Addison said, pointing at one of the bar stools on the other side of the counter from where she was stirring the rice.

"Okay," Ronni said as she walked carefully to the bar stool and sat down.

"Are you alright?" Addison asked, suddenly noticing how slowly Ronni was walking.

"She had a little mishap today," Clay said with a smile before kissing Anna Grace again.

"It was nothing, but your wonderful boyfriend here saved the day with his first aid kit," she said with a thankful smile.

"What on Earth happened?"

"Well, I sort of fell out of a tree."

"You fell out of a tree?" Addison asked, half laughing even though she was trying so hard not to. "Why do I assume my brother had something to do with this?"

Ronni shrugged her shoulders, and Clay made his way out of the kitchen as he was certain this was about to turn into "girl talk".

"Brad wanted to show me the town from a different angle, he said."

"In a tree? Good Lord. He's nuts." Addison laughed, memories of her craziest brother running through her head. He had always been into something, and their mother had gained many a gray hair from raising Brad. He'd even toilet paper rolled the hospital grounds on a dare once. There was nothing Brad Parker wouldn't do to get a laugh.

"I think he had good intentions..."

"How did you fall?" Addison asked as she poured

more seasonings into her made-up rice dish. She hoped it wouldn't choke Ronni.

"Well, I guess I didn't fall exactly. I jumped." Before Addison could respond, Ronni started laughing.

"Wow. I know my brother is a bit much sometimes, but did you really need to jump out of a tree to get away from him?" Addison giggled.

"Apparently, yes," she said, joining in the laughter.

"Listen, if there's one thing you need to know about my brother, it's that he'll do anything for a laugh… even if it means taking a woman he just met up into a tree."

"I don't think he was trying to be funny. At least he didn't seem to be."

"That's a first. Brad is serious about nothing," Addison said offhandedly.

"Oh. Really? What about… relationships?" Ronni said, trying to sound nonchalant.

"You know, Brad hasn't had a serious relationship in a while. He's always dated a lot. I mean, even though he's my brother, he seems to be fairly good looking."

Ronni said nothing. She didn't want it getting back to Brad that she thought he was more than good looking, and the thought made her mad at herself. "You mean, he's never even had a broken heart?"

Addison thought it was a strange question, but she answered it anyway. "Once, but he doesn't like to talk about it. More times than not, he might have broken some hearts along the way, but he never gets invested enough to get his heart broken anymore. Still, I hope he settles down one day. He deserves it. It's going to take one special woman to tame my brother!"

Addison's phone rang and interrupted their conversation. She excused herself to answer it, turning off the burners on the stove as she walked into the next room.

Ronni was left wondering why she cared about Brad's love life. She had no interest in her own love life anymore. That part of her was closed off. Work would have to be the love of her life, because she sure wasn't opening her heart to anyone anytime soon.

THE NEXT DAY was one of the Parker family's favorite days of the year - the 4th of July. Full of fun and festivities, Addison couldn't wait to host not only her family, but many of the townspeople, at her new B&B.

The place was decorated to the max outside, and Clay had set up multiple tables for some local vendors to offer food and crafts to the visitors. The Parker family arrived around noon, including Adele, who brought her new beau, Harrison Gibbs.

Addison and the Parker brothers enjoyed having Harrison around. He told all kinds of stories about their father, and it was good to hear those memories from someone who had known him for many years.

"Where's my baby?" Adele asked as she passed an apple pie into Addison's hands before almost pushing past her to take the baby from Clay. Addison laughed. Her mother was baby focused these days, that much was sure.

"Hello, Addison," Harrison said with a deep laugh as he bent down and kissed her on the cheek. "I'm sure your mother is happy to see you too." Adele turned around, clutching Anna Grace to her chest.

"Oh, of course, sweetie," Adele said with a smile as she whisked the baby away to the rocking chair on the large front porch of the B&B. Addison stood watching her mother love on her new granddaughter, and she was so thankful for the way things had turned out.

Coming home pregnant with another man's baby - who wasn't her husband - had been hard. She had been so embarrassed and ashamed at her behavior, but in the end it had all worked out for the best. Now she was with the love of her life, Clay, and running her new B&B. Life couldn't get any better.

RONNI SAT in her rented room in the B&B and looked out the window, being careful not to let anyone see her there. She didn't want to look like some kind of stalker, staring down at the festivities in the garden behind the house. Dozens of towns-people crowded the space, talking, laughing and eating.

Addison and Clay had both separately invited her to join the family in a 4th of July picnic, but she just wasn't feeling all that jovial today. Most people would think she was homesick or something, being away from California, but she wasn't. In fact, she was glad to be anywhere but California at the moment.

Getting to come on this business trip had been a godsend, coming along just at the right moment. Literally.

It wasn't that she didn't like living in California. She enjoyed it for the most part, but it could get lonely for a woman like her. Having no stable family to speak of and being an only child, Ronni had spent much of her life taking care of herself.

She had pulled herself up by her bootstraps, gotten her college degree and conquered the corporate world all by her mid twenties. By now, she'd have expected to have been married with kids, but things had happened that had gotten in the way. Mostly her career, but probably more than that was her personality quirks.

As she watched the Parker family interact downstairs, she longed deep in her soul for something like that. A family that laughed together. A man in her life who supported her work, but took care of her.

What kind of thing was that to say? She was an independent woman. She didn't need a man to "take care of her", yet she seemed to long for it anyway.

"Ronni?" she heard Brad say from the other side of her bedroom door as he knocked. Dang it. Why hadn't she noticed he wasn't anywhere in her bedroom window view?

"Yes?" she called back, trying to sound annoyed but really feeling giddy that he was there. What was that about?

"Can you open the door?" he asked with a laugh.

"Why?" she called back again.

"Because I feel like an idiot talking to a door." She smiled, and her heart skipped a beat. Uh oh. That wasn't good.

She walked over to the mirror, ran her fingers through her hair, which was hanging straight today, and opened the door. Brad's face changed for a moment, as if something had surprised him, and then looked into her eyes.

"Hey," she said softly.

"Hey. I just wanted to make sure you were coming down to the party…" he started, pointing behind him as if the party was happening right there.

"Oh. Actually, no…"

"What? Why not?"

"It's not really my thing, and I have so much paperwork to catch up on, Brad," she said, trying her best to pretend that she didn't have an urge to run downstairs and eat apple pie all day.

"Ronni, what's with you?" he asked, this time being more serious than she'd seen him before.

"What's that supposed to mean?" she asked, her hands on her hips like a thirteen year old girl.

"Well, correct me if I'm wrong, but you're here to

mingle with the community and get to know them so you can sell the idea of the new Lamont, but you won't come meet people. You don't smile. You don't talk. How exactly do you plan to accomplish your task? Magic?" he asked, sarcasm dripping from his voice. Ugh. She hated him again.

"I'm a little sore today, if you must know," she said, trying again to come up with a valid excuse. She walked away and sat on her bed, pulling her leg from underneath her long red skirt. Brad cringed when he saw the huge scab covering the main scrape on her leg.

"Jeez, Ronni, I'm so sorry… again," he said with a sigh as he walked over to her and sat down next to her on the bed. She tensed up.

"It's okay. I know you didn't mean to. But if it's all the same to you, I'd rather spend the day chilling out up here… alone." As she said the words, she knew she was lying to him - and to herself. She would really rather eat and laugh and smile. But she didn't deserve that. Not after what had happened back in California.

Maybe she was just punishing herself for being stupid. Or maybe she'd done the smartest thing she'd ever done. Maybe she'd never know.

"No."

"Excuse me?" she said, shocked at his decisive way of speaking sometimes. It was kind of a turn-on, unfortunately.

"I said no. You're not sitting up here."

"Um, pardon me, Brad Parker, but you don't get to dictate what I do. I'm your boss, remember?" she said as she yanked her skirt back down over her leg and stood up.

"You may be my boss on this project, but if we don't convince the community that this new attraction is a good thing, we both lose. So, I need your help. Bring your beautiful California face downstairs so we can do some preemptive PR," he said as he stood and walked toward the door. "And keep your hair down like that. It looks nice, and you look more approachable."

With that, Brad shut the door and left Ronni standing there, befuddled and confused. Why did she want to follow his instructions?

"So, where's California girl?" Kyle asked when Brad returned to the yard.

"She's coming. I hope, anyway."

"You hope?"

"I gave her an ultimatum… kind of."

"And she took you seriously?" Kyle laughed.

"I think so, actually. Of course, she's a pain in the ass, so it's hard to tell."

"Man, she's got you tied up in knots already," Kyle said as he punched Brad in the shoulder.

"No, she doesn't. She's my boss. That's it."

"Ooohhh…. Somebody's sensitive," Kyle said. Before Brad could respond, Ronni was walking across the yard. And damn, she was hot.

She was still wearing her long red skirt, likely to cover the gash on her shapely leg, but she was now wearing a form fitting white tank top too. Her long blond hair draped over her perfectly tanned shoulders, she was the most beautiful woman he'd ever seen.

"Ronni Blair, this is my brother, Kyle," Brad said as Ronni reached out and shook Kyle's hand. "He's the one who got married recently."

"Oh, congratulations," she said, a hint of something in her voice. Was it sadness?

"Thanks. How are you liking January Cove so far?"

"Well, I've only been here a few days, but it's growing on me. I've enjoyed the quiet compared to my normal fast-paced lifestyle in California."

"I bet. Oh, Jenna's waving me over," Kyle said, pointing across the yard at his new wife waving for him. "Nice to meet you, Ronni."

"And you too," she said smiling as he walked away. She looked around anxiously for a moment and then looked up at Brad. "Well, here I am, at your service. How do we woo these people? Pork rinds?"

"Was that supposed to be a Southern joke?" he asked, tilting his head.

"No. I'm sorry. That was rude."

"No surprise there…"

"Look, Brad, I'm here, okay? Just tell me what I need to do. I can't afford to lose my job, so I've got to make this work." That was one of the first honest things he'd heard her say.

"If you're serious, then let's get to work."

"How?" she asked, hands on her hips again.

"Well, you can start by being nice. And then we'll eat pie and watch fireworks…" he said, gently putting his hand on her back and leading her toward the people.

"And how will that help?"

"Because then people might think you're nice. And normal…" he said, smiling as she seethed at him.

CHAPTER 5

*T*he mornings in January Cove were almost as hot as the afternoons this time of year. July was a hot time in Georgia, but at least the constant ocean winds kept the area manageable.

Brad had been working with Ronni for over a week now, but chipping away at her outer shell had been close to impossible. Although she had made some connections at the 4th of July get-together, her tough exterior remained.

But she was smart. Super smart. Smarter than anyone he'd ever met.

Her business sense was astounding. And sexy. And irritating.

On this morning, they were scheduled to meet with the local City Council to go over the final plans for the Lamont. Brad was more "dressed up" than usual, wearing a pair of khaki pants and a navy blue golf shirt. When he spotted Ronni getting out of her car across the parking lot at City Hall, she was breathtaking.

She wore a gauzy white dress, and he could just make out the hint of her shape underneath it. Now he regretted wearing his tighter pair of pants.

"Good morning," he called to her, placing his ever-filling briefcase in front of his ever-growing…

"Good morning," she said, not a hint of a smile on her face. She was all business, as usual. "Is that a uniform of some kind?" she asked, pointing at his attire.

"Very funny."

"I thought maybe you were flipping burgers after this," she said, a hint of a smile playing across her lips. Then it was gone as soon as it came.

She carried her own briefcase, and with a determined look on her face, she barreled toward the front door. Brad grabbed her arm and pulled her to the side.

"What are you doing?" she asked, yanking her arm away.

"Don't you think you need to know a few things before you go charging in there?"

She sighed. "This town takes way more work than I anticipated."

"Look, this is small town America, Ronni. These people care about each other and what goes on here. It's been this way for generations, so you can't go in there with this big city mentality about 'change is good' because they won't buy it."

"So what do you want me to do, Brad?" she asked, her arms crossed.

"Well, first of all, uncross your arms," he said. She begrudgingly did it. "And second of all, smile. And listen to them. And open your mind and your heart to what they're saying." She finally started nodding along like she was taking mental notes. "The head of the City Council is Ben Gay."

Ronni let out a loud laugh. "Like the ointment?"

"Yes," Brad said trying not to laugh himself. "And he hates when people make fun of his name."

"He should've changed it then..."

"Not really the point right now," Brad said, rolling his eyes. "Two of the other members who have a lot of say-so in what goes on around here are Elmer Drysdale and Wilma Farmer."

"Good Lord. These names..."

"Focus, Ronni."

"Sorry. Okay, can we go in now? I think I've got

it. Ointment guy, Elmer and Wilma." He stared at her for a minute. "What?"

"I'm right there if you need me," he said, unsure of why he said it. She looked a little stunned, so he opened the door and waved her in before she could say anything.

"So, Miss Blair, what exactly does your company plan to do with our Lamont? Tear it down?" Wilma Farmer asked, her glasses pinching the end of her substantial nose.

"No, certainly not," Ronni said, standing tall as she pulled out the stack of colorful presentations she'd brought with her. Brad was impressed with her preparedness, but he wasn't sure the current audience would be so excited about the stodgy file folders. "We want to maintain the integrity of the historical value of the Lamont."

The entire room stared at her, and Brad swore he heard crickets chirping. This was not going well.

"What Miss Blair is trying to say is that she wants the locals to still feel like the Lamont is a part of their history. The plan isn't to change everything, but to add to it and showcase the history of our town," Brad said as he walked back and forth across the front of the room. Ronni looked at him, trying to hide her astonishment at his sudden ability to speak in front of a room like he'd done it a million times before. "The Lamont is important to the people of January Cove, and that's one reason Miss Blair hired me for the job. Ya'll know how much history I have at the Lamont," he said as a few of the members giggled.

"Yes, we do, Brad Parker. Do you remember when you pulled the fire alarm and cleared out the whole theater?" Elmer asked, his puffy face red with laughter.

"Yes, sir, I do. I was just trying to get a few minutes alone with Sissy Candell," he said with a crooked smile.

"Did it work?" Elmer asked, sitting forward on his chair.

"I can't kiss and tell, Mr. Drysdale," Brad said which caused a huge chuckle to come from the mostly elderly council members. From his side, Brad heard one of Ronni's famous sighs sliding from her lips. "But back to the Lamont…"

"Yes, back to the Lamont," Ronni started to say, but Brad cut her off yet again.

"The plan with the Lamont is to use it as a bridge between the locals and the tourists in January Cove.

We all know that we can't survive and grow our town without encouraging a little more tourism," he said as Wilma wrinkled up her nose and crossed her arms. She was not a fan of turning January Cove into a tourist mecca at all. She was in her seventies, and her family had practically founded the town starting with her grandfather.

"Tourism, hmmph," she snorted. Ronni's eyes were as big as saucers as she looked between Wilma and Brad for what seemed like hours.

"Now, Ms. Farmer, you know I'm telling the truth," he said, smiling at her as he leaned on her side of the table. "We want to build the botanical gardens, right?"

"Well, yes," she said, begrudgingly.

"Then we have to raise more capital, and the Lamont is our biggest asset. Having all of those tourists here can only be a boon to the economy in January Cove, but we can't do it without the support of the City Council. And that's why Miss Blair and I would like for you to all take a look at these numbers..." he said, nodding his head to Ronni as she passed out the folders.

THE SUN WAS BEATING DOWN when they finally made it back outside after the meeting. The council members left as a group, heading out to eat lunch at one of the local restaurants, which left Ronni and Brad standing outside alone.

"Okay, look, before you start yelling at me…" Brad started, fully prepared to get the onslaught of irritated comments about how he took over and didn't let her speak.

"Yelling? You think I'm going to yell at you?" she asked with a laugh. "You were fantastic in there! I could kiss you!"

Brad stopped mid-walk as they headed for their cars. "Oh yeah?"

"It was a figure of speech, but still, you were amazing in there. I didn't know you could…"

"What? Talk like a normal human?" he said with a laugh. "Yeah, I can string sentences together and everything."

"You know what I meant," she said, waving her hand at him as they reached their cars.

"No, I really don't, but it doesn't matter anyway. We've got them eating out of our hands now, and with their support the project will go a lot smoother," Brad said. "So, congratulations." He reached out his hand to shake hers, and she slipped hers into his. Her hand was soft, delicate and warm, and he didn't want to let it go. But apparently she did. "I guess I'll see you at the theater after lunch," Brad said as he turned for his truck.

"What? No celebratory lunch?" she called to him.

"You want to go to lunch with me?"

"Well, I'm hungry and it's lunch time. That would make logical sense, wouldn't it?"

"No salad today?"

"Don't that have salads at the restaurants around here?" she asked with a smile.

"I HAVE TO ADMIT, this place isn't half bad," Ronni said as she took the last bite of her clam chowder. "I don't think I've ever had better chowder, actually." Brad had brought her to The Wharf, which was one of the town's nicer restaurants, situated with a stunning ocean view.

It was nice to see her loosen up for a bit, and she was starting to feel like a friend. Or at least an acquaintance that might donate blood to him if he needed it. Maybe.

"Glad you like it. This place only opened about

RACHEL HANNA

five years ago, but it's usually hopping on the weekend nights. Not a huge lunch crowd, though."

Over lunch, they'd kept most of the talk to work related issues, but he had learned that Ronni was an only child and her mother wasn't exactly the most stable person in her life.

The rocky relationship she described between her and her father made Brad wonder if it was one of the reasons she seemed so snippy at men. Or maybe she was only that way with him.

Brad called the waitress to get the check, but the ringing of Ronni's cell phone interrupted their discussion. She looked down, and concern briefly swept across her face as she checked the screen.

"Oh. I need to take this. Do you mind....?" she asked, pointing at the check.

"My treat," Brad said as she stood up and walked to the door. Realizing he had enough cash in his pocket, he laid it on the table and walked outside to find her.

"Yes, I understand the deposit is non-refundable. Trust me, this was an unexpected turn of events," she said in a low voice from around the corner. Brad couldn't help but listen in, curiosity getting the better of him. He knew it was wrong, but he wanted

74

to know what this woman's deal was, and maybe eavesdropping would give him the details.

She continued. "I'm really very sorry. Yes, yes, I know. Please don't raise your voice with me, okay? I'm very upset too. I was supposed to be on my honeymoon right now!" she said in a high pitched whisper, and Brad's stomach dropped. Her honeymoon?

Too bad cell phones can't be slammed down because that would've given Brad an indicator that she'd hung up and was coming back around the corner where he was standing. Instead, she ran smack dab into his chest with a thud and almost fell backward.

"Brad! My God, you scared me to... Wait? Were you listening to my conversation?" Brad stood there looking like the cat that ate the canary, unable to find words for the first time in his life. "Answer me!"

"I... um... I didn't mean...." Maybe he was having a stroke, he thought. He had no words, and his thoughts were zooming a mile a minute.

"You're so infuriating! You had no right to eavesdrop on me!" she said, and he could've sworn tears were welling in her eyes before she started walking quickly back toward the parking lot. Luckily, they'd taken his truck and it was way too far to walk back to the Lamont.

"Ronni! Wait!" he called to her, surprised at how fast those lean legs of hers could move. When he caught up to her at the truck, she wasn't even out of breath and he felt like he was going to die. Note to self - need more cardio.

"Unlock my door," she said in a low growl as she stood there, her arms crossed tightly over her chest.

"I'm sorry. I really am. I came outside and heard you talking, and before I knew it, I heard you say you're supposed to be on your honeymoon right now. It wasn't intentional, Ronni. Really," he said, knowing full well that wasn't the total truth but he would rather not get strangled at the moment so he went with it.

She took in a deep breath and finally looked at him. "I guess you want the whole story?"

"Only if you want to tell me," he said softly. Sure, he wanted to know, but it was obviously painful for her.

"I guess it doesn't matter now, and it will only distract you from work if I don't tell you," she said with a hint of a smile.

"Ah, you already know me well."

"Can we walk?" she asked. He was surprised that she wasn't aching to get back to work as usual.

"Sure. Let's walk down to the beach," Brad said, pointing behind him.

They walked quietly for several minutes, only the sound of sea gulls and waves between them. When they reached the sand, she stood for a moment and breathed in deeply.

"I love the smell of the ocean," she said in almost a whisper.

"Me too." He had decided during their walk to just let her do the talking and not push although it was against his every natural inclination not to start battering her with questions.

Ronni walked over to a jagged rock near the water and sat down, pulling her long, white dress under her as she tucked her feet under one hip. Brad said down across from her, his back to the water he loved so much.

"His name is Evan."

"Evan. Got it."

"We were supposed to get married two weeks ago. Our honeymoon was going to be in Aruba this week. The call I got was from the caterer. I lost my deposit, but they want me to pay for the whole thing since they lost out on getting other events for that date."

"I see… The wedding got called off?"

"Yes. Evan called it off. My whole world was turned upside down, so I told my boss to send me somewhere… anywhere. And anywhere turned out to me January Cove."

"I'm sorry, Ronni."

"Don't pity me, Brad. I'll be fine. I'm just not meant for love," she said, a sad look spreading over her face as she stared out at the water. "And I don't like to talk about personal stuff, so I'd appreciate it if we could just leave this conversation here."

"That's not true."

"What's not true?"

"That you're not meant for love. Evan must be an idiot to have given up a woman like you, Ronni." His voice was soft, and it was taking every ounce of strength he had in him not to lean over and kiss her square on the mouth. Never had he felt such an instant attraction to a woman in his life.

"You don't really know me, Brad," she said quietly. "I can be hard to deal with sometimes."

He grinned. "No. Really? Impossible." He faked his shock by putting his hand on his heart and allowing his mouth to gape open.

She leaned over and took a hand full of sand from the ground before tossing it into his lap. "Oops, sorry. Did I mess up your uniform?"

"Oh, you're going to pay for that!" he said as she jumped up and started jogging toward the water. He chased her down, grabbing her around the waist and spinning her. When they stopped, she fell to the ground and he toppled down behind her. They both lay on their backs, staring up at the blue sky.

"You know, I'm almost kind of glad that we met," she said, so softly that he could barely hear her over the waves. He popped up onto one elbow, his mouth hanging open.

"Excuse me? I think I have sand in my ears."

She laughed and the rolled to her side too. "No, I actually said that. And I'm not sure why."

"Maybe my wonderful qualities are finally winning you over, Miss Blair," Brad said as he reached out and chucked her shoulder lightly.

"Let's just say I could use a friend right now."

"So we're friends?"

"Aren't we?"

"You just put sand on my crotch."

"Do you have to say crotch?"

"What am I supposed to call it? Because I can describe it in other ways…"

"Nevermind. That's okay," she said as she sat up and looked out at the ocean, her feet pulled close to her as her white dress blew lightly in the breeze. Brad sat up too.

"I'd be glad to be your friend, Ronni."

"You would?"

"Yes, but can you stop making it so dang hard all the time? Take off the coat of armor and trust me?"

"You caused me to fall out of a tree," she said giggling.

"And you sanded my crotch, so we're even."

"Jeez, the mental images you can conjure up…"

"Thinking of my crotch again, are you?"

She smiled slyly, all the while loading her hand up with sand again. When she pushed it down the back of his shirt and bolted toward the car, he knew he had to have this woman. Forever.

CHAPTER 6

*A*ddison could barely keep her eyes open as she leaned back in the rocking chair, Anna Grace resting peacefully on her chest. She really needed to review the week's financial report on her iPad, but her baby girl had kept her up most of the night with an earache and she just couldn't focus.

Clay had tried to help, but sometimes a baby girl needs her mommy. Or maybe it was the other way around. Sometimes the mommy needs to be in charge, and that was Addison's problem most of the time. She wasn't willing to give up control to anyone, including Clay.

Which had led to an argument.

Clay felt like she didn't think of him as Anna Grace's "real" father, and that wasn't it at all. But

Addison had been tired at the time, and her mouth had gotten the best of her… again.

"Knock knock…" she heard Jackson whisper as he walked into the nursery.

"Oh, hey, Jack…" she whispered back as she slowly stood up and placed the baby in her crib. Addison turned on the baby monitor, a high-tech thing with TV screens, and motioned for Jackson to follow her downstairs to the kitchen.

She walked straight to the coffee pot and poured a large cup. "Coffee?" she asked him. He nodded, and she poured another large cup for her brother.

"Long night?" he asked with a smile.

"That doesn't even begin to describe it," she said, sliding down onto the barstool and relishing in the first sip of coffee. Her hair was a mess, her bathrobe wrinkled and her general appearance disheveled. "I didn't know babies had lungs on them like that. She literally cried for almost three hours straight."

"Gettin' old, Addy. I stayed up til three in the morning working, and look at me." He stretched his hands across his puffed up chest and then flexed his muscles.

"Oh, you just wait, Jackson Parker," she seethed with a grin. "When Rebecca has a baby…"

"Whoa… Don't get too far ahead of yourself, sis. We're not even married, or engaged for that matter."

"Yeah, what's up with that anyway?" she asked as she topped her coffee off yet again.

"Um, that wasn't the reason for my visit today."

"No? Then why are you here?" she asked, a little more pointedly than she meant to.

"I saw Clay this morning at the dock. He looked upset."

"Did he tell you to come talk to me?" she asked, her eyebrows knitted together.

"No. He isn't that way. You know that, Addy. He's a proud man, and not one to share private stuff. But he's like an extra brother to me, and I hope things are okay with you guys."

"They'll be okay. We just had a little tiff last night. I'm sure we'll get over it soon enough," she said as she stared out at the garden behind the B&B.

"You're a terrible liar."

"I'm not lying, Jackson. We'll be fine. He just needs to be more understanding…"

"Of?"

"Fine. I'll tell you. Anna Grace has been sick with an ear infection. He wanted to care for her while I slept last night, but I wouldn't let him. He got all

83

offended, thinking I don't believe he's capable or her real father. Ridiculous."

"I agree. You are being ridiculous."

"Me?" she snipped. "He's the one..."

"Addy, come on now. This man adores you and has for most of your life. And he loves that baby like she's his own. He needs to feel needed. He needs that bonding time with her as much as you do. And he's more capable than most men I know."

She sat there staring at her brother for a minute, unsure of what to say because she knew he was right. That didn't make it any easier.

He scooted closer and put his hand on her knee. "Listen, sis, I'll tell you a little secret about us men. We all grew up watching superheroes, and we longed to be them. To leap tall buildings and fly over the highest mountains all while slaying dragons. And then women entered the picture. We wanted to impress them, slay every dragon that comes into their path. Clay wants to be your hero, and you're depriving him of that feeling. He wants to watch you sleep peacefully while he takes care of you and Anna Grace."

Her eyes welled up with tears. "Oh God, Jackson. I really screwed up. I wasn't thinking... I'm just so tired..."

"Clay will forgive you, Addy. Just tell him you understand. I think you spent so long on your own, even when you were married, that you haven't quite grasped that you don't have to do everything alone anymore."

She smiled. "Dang it."

"What?"

"You're right. And I hate when you're right."

RONNI WALKED around the edge of the conference table and leaned over Brad's head, her chiseled arm sliding across the paperwork in front of them both.

"See? That estimate is inflated. I think we can get that down by at least another fifteen percent. Don't you?" she asked. He froze in place. God. She. Smelled. Good. Like puppies and rainbows and chocolate... and all the other good things in life rolled into one. He'd been awake the last two nights thinking about her, and the sleep deprivation was getting to him. "Brad?"

"Oh, yeah, totally."

"Totally?" she said, as she stood upright and crossed her arms. "What is this? Nineteen eighty-five?"

"Sorry. I was… distracted."

"By?"

Frustrated and severely lacking sleep, he stood up and crossed his own arms, his eyes squinting at her. "Fine! I'll tell you. You're stunningly beautiful and smell like a dream, and it's extremely distracting to want to pin your co-worker against the wall and kiss her until her lips can't take another second."

Crap. Had he just said that out loud? He could only hope it was a wonderfully vivid hallucination.

"Brad…" she started.

"No, don't say another word. I don't want to hear one of your lengthy lectures about how I can't think with the head on my shoulders. Trust me, this pains me as much as it pains you, but you asked and I told you."

"Brad…"

"Stop. Seriously," he said, holding up his hand. "Let's just get back to work. And being 'friends,'" he said, using air quotes like a teenage girl.

"I'm trying to…"

"I mean, come on, how much can a guy take?" he said, now pacing around the room, running his fingers through his hair like all of the Parker men did when they were stressed. Usually by a woman. "You waltz into January Cove, all gorgeous and smart, and I haven't dated anyone in a while... I mean, it's normal, right?"

"Can I just..."

"And then there's your neck. It's like a swan. How could any man not want to kiss a neck like that? Of course, I could just go to the pond and look for a swan, but something tells me that wouldn't be the same at all..." Now he was sounding like a lunatic.

"Brad... Just listen to me..."

"And then I find out that some stupid guy named Evan actually had you ready to walk down the aisle and bailed on you? I hate all guys named Evan now, so thanks for ruining that name for me..."

Before he could say another word, she walked up and slapped him across one cheek. Shocked - and a little turned on if he was honest - he stopped talking and rubbed his cheek.

"Why'd you do that?"

"Because you wouldn't shut the hell up. Jeez. Can you take a breath now?"

"As long as I don't move my cheek, I guess," he said as he stretched his mouth from side to side to try and take out the sting.

"Good. Now, first of all, thanks for all of the compliments. A girl likes to hear those things. And secondly, maybe if you'd stop pacing like a caged lion and actually ask me out on a date, I might say yes."

Brad was sure that she'd affected his brain's abilities to process information correctly. Did she say she'd go on a date with him?

"Excuse me, what?" he asked, turning his ear toward her.

"I said I might want to go out on a date with you. If you want to, that is."

He walked toward her slowly. "Um, I think that's pretty obvious..."

For the first time, she seemed timid and almost shy as she looked down at the floor instead of him. So he knelt and took both of her hands in his. Ronni's eyes were bugging out of her head.

"What're you doing?"

"My dear Ronni, would you go on a date with me?" he asked in his best Rhett Butler accent.

"Well, I do declare, Brad Parker, I would be honored," she said, in the worst Scarlett O'Hara accent he'd ever heard. But he'd listen to it all day long if he could.

Brad stood back up and continued holding her hands. "I thought you'd say no."

"You did? Why?"

"Because we work together… and you don't like me very much."

"Well, we won't work together forever… and I like you more than you think." She winked at him and then walked out of the room, knowing full well he was watching every inch of her as she did.

"Wow, you look beautiful!" Addison said as Ronni stood in the kitchen of the B&B. "My brother's tongue is going to be hanging out. Watch your shoes for drool," she giggled as she wiped the counter with a wet cloth to clean up behind a new guest who'd come to stay that day.

The B&B was growing, and some days Addy was finding it hard to get everything done. Taking care of Anna Grace, spending time with Clay, sleeping, taking care of guests. It was a lot more than she'd expected in the beginning, but she was enjoying her life, as busy at it was these days.

"Thanks. I'm a little nervous, to tell you the truth," Ronni admitted. She was wearing a simple blue sundress and silver strappy sandals with low heels. Her long blond hair was cascading over her tanned shoulders, and she added a touch of lip gloss to her full lips just to add a fuller effect.

Truth was that she was pretty excited about her date, and that would've never seemed possible a couple of weeks ago. When she'd first met Brad, he wasn't her type at all. Southern, down to Earth, loud. She thought of herself as more reserved, a little uptight even. At least that was what she'd been told her whole life.

"Ronni's too serious."

"Ronni never has any fun."

But what was she supposed to be like when she'd been raised by what seemed to be a pack of wolves?

Her mother had had the best of intentions, she supposed. She was young herself when she had Ronni. At only seventeen years old, her mother was just a kid and didn't really know how to be a mother.

When her family pressured her to marry the father of her baby, Ronni's mother had given in and married him. But he was a bad man and very abusive to both her mother and her. Finally, when she was six years old, she and her mother escaped and went to live in a shelter for battered women and children.

It was a memory Ronni never wanted to think about. She could still see that place in her mind and smell the cigarette smoke and orange scented cleaning solution they used on the floors. It was an odd mixture of smells, and it always made her stomach churn.

When they finally got on their feet, they moved to a small apartment just outside of Baltimore. Ronni thought her mother would get it together and make better choices, but instead she had a string of men - each worse than the one before - in the apartment at all hours or the day and night.

At around thirteen years old, Ronni realized how her mother made money. She sold her body to these men with Ronni right there in the apartment. So Ronni ran away at fourteen and went to live with a distant cousin who was eighteen and trying to be an actress in Hollywood.

Turned out to be the best choice she ever made. She found people who cared about her in California. First was a woman she worked with at a local diner. Her name was Hilda Ayers, and she was in her sixties when Ronni was fifteen. But she took her in and cared for her like a mother, getting her back in school.

Ronni worked hard to keep up her grades, and eventually got into college on a full scholarship. Being serious had gotten her far in her career, but not so much in her social life. In fact, it often sucked the fun right out of her life. But she didn't know any other way.

"Nervous?" Addy asked, breaking Ronni right out of her walk down memory lane.

"Yeah. I haven't gone on a first date in a while."

"Oh, well, Brad's harmless enough," Addy said with a laugh. "I hope I'm not prying, Ronni, but I take you as someone who's been hurt before. Am I right?"

"Haven't we all?" Ronni asked as she sat on the barstool.

"Probably. I just wanted you to know that you can trust Brad. He's a good guy, even if he is my brother."

"I know. I can tell he's got a good heart."

"Just know that I don't want anyone breaking his heart again," Addy said, trying her best to sound nice but getting her point across nonetheless.

"Again?"

"Hasn't he told you?"

"Told me what?"

"Oh. Maybe I shouldn't…"

"Please, tell me. I won't say a word."

Addison sighed and walked around the counter. "Brad was engaged once. She left him at the altar. It was to be a small beach wedding about six years ago.

He was young, she was an idiot. He showed up, she didn't. It was awful. He was so embarrassed. I think it's why he makes so many jokes now. For a long time, he had this 'get them before they get me' kind of dating mentality. It's good to see him trusting a woman again and putting himself out there."

Ronni's stomach knotted up. Before she could respond, Brad came walking through the front door carrying a bouquet of red and pink roses and wearing an off-white linen shirt and navy blue shorts. He looked so handsome that Ronni's hands started shaking, so she put them behind her back as she stood up.

"Wow, you look stunning," he said softly as he walked over and handed her the roses. Addison suddenly felt like a third wheel, so she quickly rubbed her brother's arm as she passed by and went upstairs to check on Anna Grace.

"Thank you. These are lovely."

"I think Addy keeps vases in the cabinet over there," Brad said pointing to a small freestanding cabinet at the corner of the breakfast area. Ronni found one and filled it with water before placing the flowers on the table for everyone to enjoy.

"So, where are we going?" she asked, smiling shyly.

"Lots of surprises in store for you tonight, Miss Blair," he said as he jutted out his arm for her to take. "Shall we?"

"We shall," she said in her silly Southern voice again before they walked outside into the sunshine.

CHAPTER 7

*T*he first place they went was to Breakers for dinner, which gave them lots of time to chat about life. Ronni told Brad more of her checkered past than she'd anticipated, but it felt good to finally be honest with someone about everything that had happened all those years ago. And he didn't seem to judge her for it at all.

He listened, he asked questions (because he's Brad, of course, and Brad asks questions) but there was no judgment on his face. Instead, there was genuine concern and understanding.

As someone who'd lost his own father at a young age, he at least understood those feelings of absence that not having a father brought. But more than that, he seemed to accept her right where she was, faults and all.

And it terrified her.

Did she really want to go down this road again? The whole falling in love and then disappointing another person thing? The one other time she'd opened her heart to someone - Evan - it had ended in disaster. One person left holding the bag of a two-year relationship. Feelings felt, hearts torn open, future plans dashed. The whole love thing sucked, and she'd vowed never to do it again.

Nope, she'd work until she died, own cats and learn to knit.

And then Brad appeared, like a khaki beach mirage, and now everything was spiraling out of her control again.

Jeez, it was their first date. Maybe she was over-reacting. Maybe it wouldn't work out, and she wouldn't have feelings for him. Problem was, she already did.

And if it was possible, they felt stronger. They felt more uncontrollable. And she was all about control.

Dang it.

They walked toward the car after their dinner,

and she was feeling something unfamiliar in her gut. Then she realized what it was. Peace.

Brad was just this easygoing soul who wanted nothing from her except her company. He wanted to know more about her and what made her tick, but he didn't want to change it. He didn't want to change her. That was something she hadn't experienced before in her life.

"So, where are we going now?" she asked, fully aware that he had to have other plans since it was barely getting dark.

"Oh, I have my plans. Just try to relax, Ronni. Let someone else have control for a bit, okay?" he said. Any other time, she would've fired back, but the way he said it wasn't condescending or accusatory. It was reassuring. It was like someone saying "It's okay. I've got this. Don't worry because I'm taking care of you right now." And she liked it.

They climbed into his truck and he started driving toward the pier. Moments later, they were in the parking lot, but she knew the ferry wasn't running that late. Resisting the urge to ask questions, she sat quietly enjoying letting Brad be in control for a few minutes.

He parked the truck and walked around, opening her door and reaching up for her hand. She took his and stepped down onto the pavement, the sound of ocean waves crashing behind them. He stood there for a moment and looked into her eyes and then reached out and brushed a stray clump of hair from her eyes. She thought about pulling away, but she resisted that urge too.

The tension and silence in the air was almost overwhelming.

"Ready?" he whispered as he leaned into her right ear.

"Yes..." she managed to breathe out.

"Good. Come on!" he said in his regular peppy voice before he reached down and pulled her hand toward the pier.

For a moment, she'd expected him to kiss her, and she was pretty sure she'd even started closing her eyes. Hopefully he didn't notice that.

He led her down to the end of the pier where the ferry was docked and pulled open the door leading onto the vessel.

"Is Clay here?" she finally asked as they boarded the empty boat.

"No. Why? Did you want him to be?" Brad said with a laugh as he continued pulling her forward.

"Well, no… But I don't think we should be on the ferry if he's not…" she started to say, but her words failed her when they arrived on the back of the ferry in the open area.

There were lights strung across the railing all the way around in a semi-circle. Soft music was playing in the background and a bottle of wine with two glasses sat on a small table at the corner of what appeared to be their own personal dance floor.

"You did this?" she asked, her hand over her heart as if it might jump out at any minute.

"I had a little help, but yeah, the idea was mine," he said with a wink as he finally dropped her other hand and gave her a moment to take it all in. "I wanted to go to the island but since it's dark and I don't know how to drive this thing, I figured we were safer here."

She smiled. No one had ever done something so romantic for her. Sure, Evan had proposed at a restaurant in front of a crowd, but it was so staged and stereotypical that it didn't even affect her like this old ferry boat in January Cove did.

"I don't know what to say…" she stammered as she listened to one of her favorite Michael Buble songs piping through the speaker in the corner.

"You don't have to say anything, Ronni," Brad said softly as he stood a few inches in front of her. "May I have this dance?"

Her face started to feel flush, as if she'd been transported back to eighth grade when Stevie Carrigan asked her to dance at their spring formal. Only Brad didn't have raging acne and a lisp.

"I'd be delighted," she said as she reached out her hand and took his again. It felt comfortable and warm and real, and she worried that she might never want to let his hand go again.

He pulled her closer, until their chests were touching, and she could feel the beating of his heart. If the force of it was any indication, he was either very nervous or needed to see a cardiologist pronto. Since she didn't know CPR, she was hopeful that it was just his nerves.

"You know," he said as they started to sway, one of his hands slipped around her waist and the other holding her hand. "You really impress me, Ronni Blair."

"I do?"

"You do."

"And why is that?" she asked softly, trying not to dig for compliments but aching to hear them.

"You're beautiful, funny when you want to be…"

"Like when I randomly fall out of trees?" she said with a giggle. Wait, did she just giggle? Ugh. This was bad.

"You didn't fall. You jumped."

"Touche... So, you were saying?" she said, still fishing for the end of the compliment.

"You're stunning, of course, but aside from the ravishing good looks that God gave you," he said with a grin, "you're super smart. And after the past you experienced, it just amazes me that you succeeded the way you have. Most people would've given up and given in, but you didn't."

It felt nice to have someone acknowledge all of her hard work. The truth was, she could've been like her mother and most of her family members. But she fought, very hard at times, to make something of herself. While she wasn't perfect, she was successful and happy most of the time, except when it came to relationships. Many men in her life had certainly failed her, that much was for sure.

"Thank you" was all she could manage to say. She was still all too aware of his presence around her, his breath lightly caressing her cheek, his heart still pounding off beat from the music.

"Do you like it here?"

"You mean January Cove?" she asked. He nodded. "It's certainly starting to grow on me." Brad smiled.

"The town or the people in it?"

"Both," she said, finally daring to look into his

eyes. They were a deep blue, much like the ocean around them, and she could easily get lost in them for hours. But there were other handsome features about Brad Parker. The beginnings of crows feet around his eyes, evidently from a lifetime of laughter. The fullness of his lips and the perfectly straight, white teeth that his mother must have sold a few houses to pay for. He had a square, strong jaw and a slightly crooked nose that was just perfect for his face.

Oh no. She was falling hard. And fast. And it wasn't good. But she couldn't seem to stop it.

"You okay? You looked a little panicked for a moment there," he asked, crouching down a bit to meet her eyes again.

"Yeah. I'm fine. Just thought of some paperwork I needed to send back to corporate tomorrow…" she lied. The last thing Brad Parker needed to know was how she was aching to kiss him on those full lips of his.

They swayed quietly to a couple of songs before Brad asked if she wanted to take a break and have some wine. They sat down on one of the benches lining the deck and watched the moonlight glimmer off the water.

"Can I ask you something?" Brad finally said,

breaking the silence. It was the longest she'd ever heard him go without talking.

"Sure…"

"What reason did he give?"

"Who?"

"Evan." Hearing his name made her tense up immediately, and she wasn't prepared to talk about it yet.

"Brad…"

"I'm sorry. I shouldn't pry. Nevermind."

"No, it's okay. I'm just not ready to talk about it, if that's okay."

"I understand," he said, instinctively reaching over and touching her bare leg. The feel of his strong, warm hand on her knee gave her chills and the bumps that sprang up all over her were visible within seconds. "Are you cold? Jeez, I'm sorry, Ronni. It's getting a little cool out here," he said looking around.

"I'm fine," she responded, hoping that he didn't realize her chills were from the heat building inside of her and not from the cool ocean breeze.

"Want to go back to my place?" he asked, an innocent question but one that she wasn't prepared to hear. She knew that if she went back to his place, it would be all over. She'd never be able to say no, never be able to deny herself the pleasure of spending the night with this man.

"Brad, I…"

"Ronni, it's okay. I'm not asking you to stay over or do anything. I just thought we could watch some cheesy movie and drink a cup of coffee. I promise, I'm not expecting anything from you. Okay?"

She looked at him and smiled, thankful that he couldn't see the somewhat dirty images floating through her own mind at the moment. How had she been so mean to this guy when she came to town? He was like a knight in shining armor, and she had never met anyone like him before. Too bad she was a wolf in sheep's clothing.

ADELE WALKED around the kitchen island and slid her hands around Harrison's shoulders. Their newly blossomed love affair had been one of the greatest surprises of her life, at least the second half of her life.

Losing her husband over two decades ago had almost killed her, but finding love again had re-awakened her in a way that she'd never imagined. It was a true gift that she intended to be grateful for.

"So, when do you think we should tell them?" Harrison whispered between kisses down her neck.

"Mmm…. This weekend? At our Sunday dinner?" she said, referring to the big family meal she had planned for the upcoming weekend. It was a good time to get all of the siblings and their mates together, but also a great way to see Anna Grace for a few hours. If she could get Addy to let someone else hold the baby, that was.

"Think they'll be shocked?"

"They'll be stunned, honey. But I hope they'll be happy for us."

"Me too."

BRAD PULLED up to his house, a smaller cottage style place around the corner from his mother's home. Being that he was the only unattached sibling now, he was glad to be near his Mom for the good home cooking and the ability to check on her from time to time.

She was independent, but he worried about her the same. His father would've expected nothing less. Of course, she seemed pretty mesmerized with

Harrison Gibbs these days, so his "checking on her" was getting to be less and less.

"This is your place?" Ronni said as he opened her car door.

"Yep. Sorry if it's a disappointment. It's a little... cozy," Brad said with a laugh. "But most bachelor pads are, I guess."

"No, it's adorable! I love it," she said as she walked to the front porch and rubbed her hand across the intricate woodwork.

"Come on in," Brad said as he opened the door and waited for her to pass through. God, she smelled good, he thought as she passed.

He flipped on the lights and went to start a pot of coffee as she looked around the living room. The walls were painted a pale yellow, which was surprising for a bachelor pad. The house had a fireplace, strange for a beach cottage, but probably useful during the coldest days of winter.

She looked at the family pictures lining one wall, and a pang of jealously flowed through her. She often wished that her formative years had been filled with good times with siblings she didn't have, but instead her story had turned out differently. Over the years, she'd gotten better about not dwelling on what she didn't have, but it still hurt sometimes.

"Whatcha looking at?" Brad asked as he came up behind her. His body was close to hers again, and it would only take one step to turn around and kiss him. But what would he think of her? That she was a slut? That she was desperate? That she'd just had a missed wedding and was already obsessing over him? There was no good outcome to her kissing him right now.

"Oh, just looking at your family pictures. They're all so happy. Is this your mom?" Ronni had somehow missed meeting Adele at the 4th of July festivities.

"Yep, that's the one and only Adele Parker. Best mom ever," he said as he leaned in, his head now just over her right shoulder.

"She's beautiful."

"Yes, she is. Listen, we're having a family brunch this Sunday, and I'd like to invite you as my guest."

She turned around, their faces now extremely close. Brad breathed in sharply, as if he was a deer caught in headlights and looked into her eyes. Ronni swallowed and then stepped back a few inches, aching for space between them before she did something stupid. Fun, but stupid.

"I appreciate the offer..." she started to say, but he put his index finger over her lips.

"No strings attached. It's just that I'm getting

tired of attending these family functions alone, Ronni. It's embarrassing. Everyone, including my mother, has someone. Except me. Poor lonely Brad," he said with a chuckle. "Help a guy out?"

She stood there, considering his request for a few moments. How could Brad Parker possibly be single? The women in January Cove were either very stupid or very blind.

"Okay."

"Okay? Really?" he asked, seemingly incredulous at her response.

"Okay," she said with a smile. Before she could stop him, he hugged her tightly. Her face was now pressed into his chest, and she thought for a moment that biting him lightly might be a great idea, but her logical mind took over before she made a fool of herself.

Slowly, he let go, and she couldn't help but feel sad.

"So, you wanna watch a movie?"

"Sure…"

They spent the next two hours drinking coffee and only half watching some stupid sci fi movie that Brad ordered on demand. They were like old friends now, and it was nice and strange all at the same time.

Ronni stretched, the official symbol for "I'm

tired, take me home" and Brad immediately got the message.

"Ready to go?" he asked. She nodded and yawned, a genuine sign of a very long day.

"Please."

"Hope I didn't bore you too much tonight. I know you come from that exciting California lifestyle."

Ronni laughed. "Yeah, I wasn't a big party animal there either. I'm more of a worker bee."

"No… Really?" he said as she chucked him on the shoulder for his sarcastic comment.

A few minutes later, and they were standing in front of the B&B. They had decided to walk there since it was just around the corner anyway. Most places in January Cove were so close that one could easily walk it. That was the beauty of a small town.

"Thank you for a wonderful night," she said softly as they stood in front of the white picket fence in front of the walkway.

"No, thank you. It was a great night," Brad said back. He had no idea what to do. It was like high school all over again, except in high school he knew if the girl liked him or not. At the moment, he needed a lie detector test to determine Ronni's feelings for him.

"See you tomorrow?"

"I would think so or else you'll fire me, right?"

She laughed. "You bet your ass I will."

And with that, she turned and walked toward the house. He watched her for a moment before turning himself, but then something overtook him. He couldn't help it. A man could only take so much.

He jogged back to the B&B and reached her before she made it to the stairs.

"Ronni?" he said, out of breath.

She turned, an expectant look on her face. Before she could say no, he pulled her close and searched her eyes for a split second, looking for any sign of her pushing him away. She didn't seem to be, so he went for it. He was all in this time. No going back.

He pressed his lips to hers, and he could feel her body go limp in his for a moment, almost like one of those women in the old movies who appeared to lose their leg strength when a man kissed them.

A small moan escaped her lips as she ran her fingers through his hair. That was a good sign, right? He was half paying attention to her kiss and half worrying that she might slap him at any moment now. Maybe she'd had too much wine, he worried, but hours of coffee would've negated that.

"I have to ask," he said through quick breaths as he pulled away for a moment.

"What?" she breathed back, her lips ready to land on his again.

"Are you mad that I kissed you?"

"Do I seem mad?" she asked with a seductive smile before she grabbed his head and pulled him toward her.

They walked sideways to get shelter from any prying eyes and leaned against the large magnolia tree in the front yard.

"My God, you're a fantastic kisser," he said as he slid his lips over her neck.

"You're not so bad yourself..." she said, her head falling backward to give him better access.

"I've never done this with my boss before," he said. "Of course, my bosses have always been men..."

"Brad?" she said, stopping him with her index finger over his lips. "Shut up, okay?"

He laughed and pulled her close again, and the night wore on as they exhausted themselves under the magnolia tree.

CHAPTER 8

*R*ebecca stood there staring at her son. He was leaving soon for a three week trip with the local church youth group, and she was going to miss him. Still, he was getting involved and that was a good thing. Leo had had a hard time fitting in after they moved from New York, but her relationship with Jackson Parker had changed all that.

Jackson had changed everything about her life, actually. After losing her husband in the September 11^(th) attacks, she'd decided to remain alone forever, but Jackson wasn't having any of that.

He'd been a wonderful role model to Leo and the perfect partner for her. She loved her life in January Cove, and everyday it was only getting better.

"Mom, I'll be fine. We're only going to West Virginia."

"I know, but I'm your mother and it's still hard."

He was going with his youth group to volunteer in some underprivileged areas, and she was so proud of him. He was growing up into a man, and Jackson was showing him what kind of man to be.

They spent a lot of time together throwing the football and fishing. Leo finally had a father to call his own, and it was a blessing.

Jackson had started mentioning their future a lot lately, but Rebecca wasn't sure. She'd never seen herself as married again, but she knew that wasn't logical or practical. She wanted to be with Jackson for the rest of her life, but she felt almost like she was betraying her husband's memory by walking down that aisle with another man.

Again, not logical, but logic has little place when it comes to emotions.

"Okay, it's time to go eat," Rebecca said after being lost in thought for a few minutes.

"Where's Jackson?"

"He'll meet us at the Parker house," Rebecca said as she grabbed her purse and they headed for the Sunday brunch.

"WELCOME, WELCOME..." Adele said as her children walked through the door one by one.

Everyone was there, and she loved it. Having them all together was precious to her, but that would soon change and she wasn't sure how anyone would take it.

"Hey, Mom. What smells so good in here?" Aaron asked as he and Tessa hugged Adele.

"My pot roast and homemade apple pie," Adele said, and Aaron's mouth immediately began to water for his mother's famous cooking.

"Hey, Mama Adele," Clay said as he walked through the door with Addison closely behind holding her prized little girl. Adele immediately reached for her, and this time she won as Addy let the baby go.

"Wow, I can't believe it..." Adele muttered as she walked away with her granddaughter in tow.

"Hello, Parker people!" Brad yelled from the doorway with Ronni on his arm. Everyone stared for a moment, but Brad shot them a look of warning.

"Hey, sweetie," Adele said as she hugged her son. "And you must be Ronni?"

"I am," Ronni said with a smile. Adele pulled her

into a side hug and welcomed her.

"See? They're not so bad," Brad whispered to her.

"I never said they were bad."

"No, but you were scared. They'll love you like I…" he said and then stopped himself. What an idiot. What kind of guy professes his love in such a short period of time… to his boss?

"Excuse me?"

"Hey, do you like pie?" he said, changing the subject as he tried to pull her to the kitchen.

"Brad, what did you say?" she asked again.

"I misspoke. It's okay. Don't panic."

She stood there, cocked her head to the side and took a deep breath before looking at him. "That's the thing. It didn't panic me."

With that, she walked away into the kitchen and started talking to Addison. The question was, did it panic Brad?

AFTER LUNCH, the family retired to the screened porch to have coffee and dessert. Everyone was talking and laughing, as usual, but Brad could tell his mother was tense.

She was fidgeting and kept whispering to Harrison, and Brad was worried. What if her health was failing again? The mild stroke she'd had a year ago was always on his mind, and he didn't want her to stress out.

Finally, she cleared her throat.

"Can I have everyone's attention for a minute?"

The kids all stopped talking and looked at Adele. When she demanded attention, she got it.

"I have an announcement to make, and I thought doing it today made the most sense because we're all here together."

"Mom, you're scaring me. Is everything okay?" Addison asked, bringing up what everyone was thinking.

"My health is fine, so no worries about that." A collective sigh of relief was audible throughout the room. "But this is big news, and I hope you'll all take it as good news... because I do." Brad noticed his mother sending a knowing smile toward Harrison Gibbs, and he was sure this was about the two of them and not just her alone.

"Don't leave us hanging, Mom," Jackson said, crossing his arms and smiling.

"Okay. Ya'll know that Harrison and I have enjoyed spending time together," she started as she tenderly placed her hand on his shoulder. He sat in the chair beside where she was standing, her small frame still a large presence in the room. "A few days ago, Harrison proposed." She grinned as big as Brad had ever seen, and it filled him with joy that his mother would finally have a partner in life. She deserved it more than anyone he knew.

The room erupted in congratulations and laughter and hugs, but Adele wasn't finished. "Wait… wait! That's not all…"

"You're not pregnant, are you?" Aaron said, which garnered a huge round of laughter.

"You sure would feel funny if I answered yes to that question, my dear son, but no. I'm certainly not pregnant!" she giggled. "But this might be even bigger. I'm leaving January Cove."

"What?" Jackson almost yelled, probably because he'd uprooted his life in Atlanta by staying in January Cove for his mother. Well, sort of. He'd also found the love of his life, and he certainly wasn't leaving her.

"I know this is a shock to all of you, but Harrison and I want to spend our later years getting to do all of those things we never got to do while we were raising kids. We want to travel and see things. I haven't been on a vacation in years, and it's just time."

"But what about Anna Grace?" Addison couldn't help but say. She felt terribly guilty for it, but she wanted her daughter to know her mother.

"Oh, sweetie, we'll come visit. I promise. I would never miss out on seeing her grow up!"

"What about the real estate company?" Jackson asked.

"Well, I was sort of hoping my sons might team up and take my place..." she said coyly.

"Mom..." Jackson said.

"I know, I know... You're all busy. But maybe you could run things just until I can sell the company?"

"I guess we could do that," Kyle finally piped in as he pulled Jenna close to his side. He couldn't begrudge his mother for wanting to finally live her life. She'd spent her whole life raising kids alone, and all of those dreams she'd had with their father had gone by the wayside because of it. Now was her time.

"Well, I for one admire you for doing this, Adele. It's courageous to start a whole new life at any age, and I respect you for it," Ronni suddenly heard herself saying. "Sorry. I shouldn't have spoken out. I know this is a family thing..."

"No, honey, I appreciate it. And if you're here with a son of mine, you're already part of the family.

My boys only bring home the best," she said smiling. Brad's face turned red, but Ronni's might have been even redder.

"So, what's the plan from here?" Kyle asked.

"Harrison and I are going to the Justice of the Peace tomorrow."

"What?" Jackson said a little more forcefully than he meant to.

"No need to wait at our age," Harrison said with a smile. There were a few muffled laughs from the kids.

"True story," Brad said.

"Anyway… After we get married, we plan to rent a motorhome for a couple of months and travel up the East coast. Go wherever the wind takes us," Adele said as she smiled sweetly at Harrison. Brad had never seen his mother so happy, and it was good to see.

"Well, congratulations to you both," Jenna said as she walked over and hugged Adele tightly. "No one deserves it more than you."

The family spent a lot of time together for the rest of the day, recounting old stories and laughing a lot, as they usually did. Ronni seemed to fit in well, spending a lot of time talking to Rebecca and Tessa.

"She seems nice," Jenna said as she appeared beside Brad and slipped her arm through his.

"She's very nice…"

"Oh, so tight lipped, by wonderful brother-in-law," she giggled.

"For once, right?"

"Yeah, you've never been known for your quiet nature."

"Well, she sometimes takes my ability to speak away."

"Uh oh. I think you might be in love."

"Jenna, I've only known her a couple of weeks. Don't jump the gun," he said with a smile, but without making eye contact.

"You Parker men are the worst liars…" she said under her breath as she walked away. Brad was afraid she just might be right. He'd never felt this way about any woman, including the one he was set to marry at one time.

"Well?" Ronni said as she took Jenna's place at his side.

"Well what?" he asked, worried that she'd heard his conversation with Jenna. His stomach knotted up.

"What do you think?" Her expectant look was not what he anticipated. She looked hopeful and happy and not at all irritated by what she'd obviously heard.

"Um... It seems like a good thing, right? I mean love is always a wonderful thing to experience... I think..." he was rambling now. He looked into her beautiful eyes, and she continued smiling.

"Of course I think so! New beginnings always make me smile."

"Really?"

"Brad Parker, do you think I'm so cold hearted that hearing these professions of love wouldn't warm my heart a bit?" she asked as she inched up and put her hands on his chest.

"You surprise me every minute, Ronni Blair," he whispered into her ear. She jumped a bit and he swore he heard her moan as his lips brushed against her earlobe.

She leaned back and smiled at him. "I'm happy for them. I think it's wonderful."

"Them? Who?" he asked, suddenly confused by their conversation.

"Your Mom and Harrison, of course. I thought that's who we were talking about..." she said before her face changed and she stepped back. "Wait..."

"Hey, you want some of those little mini quiche things? They're like egg pies... really good... with bacon and cheese, I think…" he said as he started to walk away. She grabbed his arm and pulled him back. For such a thin woman, she sure had great upper body strength.

"Brad, were you talking about us?" she whispered as she pulled him around the corner and out of sight.

"Seriously, if I don't get some quiche now, I'm just going to leave." What the heck was he saying?

"Brad." She said his name in a similar fashion to how his ninth grade teacher, Mrs. Sykes, used to say it. He hated that woman, but right now he would kiss her full on the lips if she'd drop from heaven and save him.

"What?"

"Were you talking about loving… me?" she asked softly without breaking eye contact.

He took a deep breath in and then let it out as he stared up at the ceiling. "And what if I was?"

"Well, that would be crazy, for one thing. We barely know each other!" her whisper was more of a hushed yell, but she didn't seem angry. She seemed incredulous, maybe, but not angry.

"And how long do we need to know each other?" he asked, finally making eye contact. He genuinely wanted to know the answer.

"Excuse me?"

"Well, just tell me when I can consider the option of loving you." He pulled out his iPhone for effect and opened the calendar. "Is late August good for you? No? Too soon? What about Halloween?"

"Quit being an idiot," she said as she pushed his phone down away from between them.

"Impossible."

"True story."

"See? You 'get' me, Ronni Blair," he said as he slipped his hands around her waist and pulled her into one of the spare bedrooms on the main floor. He locked the door behind them.

"What are you doing? Your whole family is out there!" she said without making any real attempt to escape the situation.

"I'm aware of the location of my family..." he said through kisses down her neck.

"Brad..." She was trying to have rational thoughts, but his lips were making it extra hard.

He stopped long enough to put his hands on both of her cheeks. "Ronni, I'll admit it. I've fallen madly in love with you, and it makes no sense. You've irritated me since day one, but I knew the first moment I saw you that I couldn't live my life without you. Now, this profession of love might make you think I'm desperate or crazy, and maybe you'll run away and file a restraining order against me, but I think you feel the same way."

"I..."

He put his finger over her lips. "And you don't have to say a thing. I don't need to hear it. I just need you to know how I feel, okay?" He leaned down and looked at her eye to eye.

"You make no sense to me, Brad Parker... But I won't be filing a restraining order because I'd break it over and over again to be with you," she said, grabbing his collar and pulling his lips to hers.

Unfortunately, Brad had no idea that secrets were about to be revealed and things weren't always what they seemed.

AARON DROVE up to his small cabin in the campground he ran and stood for a moment staring at the front door. Inside were his two favorite people, Tessa and Tyler. The love of his life and... the other love of his life. He couldn't imagine not having his son, and a blood relationship just didn't matter to him.

Not that he didn't want to make a whole bunch

of beautiful babies with Tessa one day, or at least do a lot of "trying".

After a hard day at work, his favorite thing was to come home, wrap his arms around her waist and kiss the crook of her neck. She always smelled like a mixture of the ocean and chocolate chip cookies, both of which were two of his other favorite things.

"Well, hello..." he said as he slipped his arms around her waist. Tyler was passed out asleep on the sofa that was pushed against one wall of their small cabin. Cartoons were on the TV, as usual, and a juice box sat perched on the edge of the sofa that Kyle had given them as a hand-me-down a few months ago.

"Hey there, my sexy man," she said, as she always did, before she turned around and gave him one of those kisses that still made his legs weak.

"Whatcha cooking?" he asked after noticing a little smoke coming from the oven.

"Dang it!" Tessa yelped. She grabbed a hot pad and opened the oven door. Smoke billowed out, and it wasn't long before the smoke alarm started blaring. This woke Tyler up, of course, and he started crying out of fear.

For a moment, Aaron stood there taking in the scene. His girlfriend running around like a headless chicken holding something that was big and black in a pan. Tyler was crying, and that was the only thing that broke him out of his daze.

"This blessed oven cooks so much faster than it should. Dinner is ruined," she sighed.

Tyler pulled her into a hug. "It's okay. I know somewhere we can go for dinner."

"I'm not dressed for going out," she said, looking down at her casual t-shirt and jeans.

"The place I'm taking you has a very 'homey' feel anyway. Come on, get Tyler and let's go!"

Within minutes, they were in the car and heading across town. Aaron wouldn't tell her where they were going, and she'd tried every restaurant in town anyway.

"Can you please tell me where we're going?" she asked once again. Aaron just smiled and squeezed her leg.

"Nope."

A moment later, they were pulling up in a very familiar driveway. Tyler bounded out because he knew exactly where they were.

"We're eating at your mother's again?"

"Sort of."

"You're giving me a headache, Aaron Parker," Tessa said with a half hearted laugh. "I really wasn't up for this tonight. I've got a load of laundry to take to the laundromat before we run out of towels and..."

"Tessa... Trust me. Okay?" She smiled, and as usual it melted his heart.

"Okay."

They got out of the car and walked inside, where Tyler was already playing with his stash of toy cars in the floor of the foyer.

"Tyler, be careful. You don't want to scratch up Grandma's beautiful floors...." Tessa said as she patted the top of his head. Adele was nowhere to be found. "Where's your Mom?"

"She's off with Harrison getting supplies for their big road trip."

Noticing the empty kitchen with no food, Tessa was confused. "Okay.... I thought we were having dinner?"

"We are if you're cooking something," Aaron said as he sat on the bar stool. "I can help, of course."

"So you brought us across town to borrow your mother's kitchen?"

"Nope. I brought us across town to use our new kitchen."

Tessa furrowed her eyebrows and leaned across the bar. "What are you up to, Aaron?"

He stood and met her on the other side of the

bar. "Tessa, my mother gave me this house today." He held up a set of keys, and tears welled in Tessa's eyes.

"What?" she managed to breathe out. "But I don't understand…"

"She's not going to be here to care for it, and she certainly doesn't need a house this large anyway. She wanted to give it to one of the kids who could use it. Kyle and Jenna already have a house and Jackson doesn't need anything right now since he's back and forth to Atlanta. She thought it would be a great place to start our marriage…"

"Well, I'm so thankful that she… wait, what?"

Before she could say another word, Aaron was on one knee right there in the kitchen.

"Tessa, would you do me the honor of becoming my wife?" he asked softly. She held her hand to her chest and sobbed.

"Yes, of course!" Aaron slipped the ring on her finger and stood. She hugged him tightly, still crying and laughing at the same time.

"Mommy, what's wrong?" Tyler asked from around the corner of the bar.

"Oh, sweetie, nothing's wrong. In fact, everything is right!" she said as she scooped him up and put him in the middle of their group hug.

CHAPTER 9

*B*rad's days were spent desperately trying to concentrate at work while Ronni milled about doing her own work. Leaning into documents, he could smell her perfume. Watching her walk around the job site in those tight skirts and high heels. Man, her calves were divine.

He had a feeling that she was just as conflicted as he was. So far, they hadn't given in to any of those desires at work, but the same couldn't be said for night time. They spent every waking hour together, only breaking apart long enough to go to their separate homes to sleep.

The more he knew about her, the more he loved her. It was crazy, but maybe it was fate. Maybe she'd been the one God had planned for him all along. He just had to wait for her, and now she was here. Like a prize at the bottom of a cereal box.

But he was all too aware that she was still planning to go home at the end of this assignment. She had a life there. Friends, a job, a home. The thought pained him more than he could express in words. Maybe he would go with her? After all, his mother was hitting the road with Harrison soon. He was free to do what he wanted now that his mother would be taken care of. Why not follow her back to Cali?

Because he loved January Cove too. It was his home, and there was no place else on Earth that appealed to him as much as his hometown. He was one of those lucky souls who got to spend his life in his personal paradise.

Maybe he would ask her to stay with him? But wasn't that way too soon? He didn't want to scare her off, but he didn't want to appear uncaring either.

"Hello?" Ronni said, waving her hand in front of his face as he sat at their makeshift conference table.

"Sorry. I was just…"

"Lost in thought?" she said with a giggle. "Yeah, I could see that. Everything okay?" She slid into the chair across from him and he reached across the table to hold her hands.

"I don't want you to leave." It was the most honest he'd ever been with any woman. Vulnerable and bare. And highly uncomfortable for him. He might as well have been naked walking down the middle of main street.

"What?"

"When this job is over. I don't want you to leave."

"But, Brad… I have a home in California. And my dream job…"

"And I can't ask you to let all of that go for me. But I wanted you to know. My heart literally aches thinking about it," he said, vulnerable yet again. Dang it. What was this woman doing to him?

She stood and walked around the table, sliding sideways onto his lap with her arms around his neck. She kissed him tenderly, the first time she'd shown that side of herself while they were on the job site.

"I don't want to go either, Brad, but this is very new. These feelings, this thing between us… I can't give up my whole life without knowing…"

"Don't finish that sentence. I know it wasn't fair of me to say that."

She put her hands on his cheeks and smiled. "No, I'm glad you did. It was the nicest thing anyone has ever said to me."

He returned her smile and leaned in to kiss her before hearing someone clear their throat in the doorway.

"Excuse me, love birds," Aaron said with a low chuckle.

Ronni shot up like a rocket and Brad sighed. His stinking brothers always ruined things for him.

"Dude, you have horrendous timing," Brad said, standing up and punching his brother in the arm.

"Well, I'm sorry. Just thought you might like to know that I wanted you to be my best man."

"What?" Brad said, momentarily confused and still a little aroused.

"Surprise!" Tessa said, jumping out from behind the doorframe. She held out her left hand to showcase the modest diamond ring that now adorned the most important finger.

"Seriously? Wow! Congratulations, you guys!" Brad said, genuinely happy for his brother and Tessa. That woman had been through the ringer in her life, and Aaron adored her.

They spent the next few minutes hugging, the two women already discussing wedding details. Tessa wanted a fall wedding, so they were planning on early October, but they would move into the Parker home immediately.

"I'm so happy for you, Tessa," Ronni said as the two women chatted over to the side. The brothers were laughing and talking loudly, as brothers sometimes do.

"Thank you. This has been a long time coming. I never thought I'd find a man like Aaron. Someone who would accept Tyler as his own, ya know? Such a blessing," she said, stars seeming to leap from her eyes as she looked at him from across the room.

"Yeah. I know what you mean..." Ronni said, although she didn't understand the full extent of it, of course. She had no children of her own, but she hoped to one day. If she ever found Mr. Right. But, wait. Maybe she had found Mr. Right.

Brad was unlike any guy she'd ever met or dated back in California. And moments ago, he was pledging his love for her and wishing she didn't have to leave soon. Why on Earth was she saying she wanted to go home? She didn't want to go back to California! The sudden realization almost made her run across the room into his arms, but she refrained.

"So I'm thinking that the weather will still be nice enough then... Don't you?" Tessa asked, obviously in the middle of a sentence. Trying not to be rude, Ronni nodded along as if she'd been paying attention the whole time.

"Absolutely."

"I know how hard it is to pay attention when one of the Parker brothers is around," Tessa whispered as she leaned in to Ronni's ear. Ronni smiled and started to turn red.

"I'm not even going to deny it."

"You and Brad… you've really developed something quickly, huh?"

"We have," Ronni said, beaming as if she'd just gotten engaged. "But, it's scary, you know?"

"Of course. It was hard for me to trust again… after what had happened to me and Tyler. But sometimes you just know it's the right thing. Being with Aaron is like… home. That's the best way to describe it. Wherever he is, that's home to me."

"Aw, baby, that was so sweet," Aaron said as he snuck up behind her and slid his arms around her waist. Brad moved to stand beside Ronni and smiled.

"Well, we'd better go. Tyler is at Adele's house, 'helping her pack'. I'm sure he's doing nothing but getting in the way!" Tessa said with a giggle. "Bye, ya'll!"

Moments later, it was just the two of them again, and Ronni was glad because she had a plan.

"So, are you busy tonight, Mr. Parker?"

"Every night can be totally devoted to you, Miss

Blair. Just agree not to go back to California…" he said in a singsongy voice as he slipped his arms around her waist and kissed her forehead.

"Let's not talk about that right now, okay? I just want to concentrate on the time we have together. This job is well underway, so I thought we could take the night off."

"Oh, my boss is so nice…" he said as he kissed up her neck.

"Brad… We have to get back to work…"

"So bossy," he said with a laugh. But he knew they had deadlines to meet, and the last thing he wanted to do was get her trouble with her bosses. Although getting her fired might spur her to move to January Cove, it probably wasn't the best way to win her heart.

JACKSON FIDDLED with the parts on the back of the refrigerator, mainly trying to look helpful and manly, but he had no idea what he was doing. Real estate contracts were his thing, but fixing an old refrigerator wasn't.

"See anything that looks broken?" Rebecca asked, craning her head around the look at him.

"Well, you see this piece right here?" Jackson said, pointing to some silver piece of metal.

"Yeah…"

"I have no idea what it does." Rebecca started laughing.

"You're quite the handyman, Jackson Parker. Why did you pull this out like you knew what you were doing?"

Jackson stood up and walked back around to the side of the fridge that he knew how to operate. "I kind of wanted you to think I was a refrigerator repairman stud…" he said as he kissed up her neck to her ear.

"Oh… like a little role playing?" she asked. He picked her up and she squealed as he tossed her on the couch like a rag doll. She screamed and squealed so much that her new cashier ran upstairs from Jolt and banged on the door.

"Miss Rebecca, are you okay?" the teenage girl yelled.

"Yes, Olivia, I'm fine! Sorry! I just tripped over something!" Rebecca called back. Olivia quickly went back downstairs to man the coffee shop.

"Oops," Jackson said laughing.

"You're terrible!"

"Hey, you're the one who screamed!"

"I love the convenience of living above my shop, but I really wish I had a place that was a little more private," Rebecca said as she stood to head into the kitchen.

"Well, then why don't you move?" Jackson asked as he followed her like the lovesick puppy that he was.

"You know I can't afford that, Jackson. The shop is just starting to break even now, and this place is free."

"You could rent it out, you know. It has that back entrance, so the tenant wouldn't even have to come up through the shop. And you could lock the door at the bottom of the stairs so they can't access it outside of business hours."

"Still, I couldn't afford renting a place right now. College is coming up soon for Leo, and I've got to sock away every bit of money I have until then."

"Rebecca, would you consider moving in with me?" Jackson asked, an expectant smile on his face.

"I don't know… That's a big step…" Her hesitation worried him.

"Let me ask you something. Where do you see this going?" he asked, pointing between the two of them.

Rebecca sighed, then smiled and took his hands. "I can't imagine my life without you. You know that."

"Then what are we waiting for? Leo is like a son to me now, and I want to be here everyday. I want the last thing I see before I fall asleep every night to be your sweet face, and I want the first thing I see when I wake up to be that crazy hair of yours…"

"Way to ruin a romantic moment!" she said as she slapped him playfully on the arm.

"Seriously, though… I don't want to push you into something you don't want…"

"I want this," she said softly. "It's just scary. It's always just been me and Leo."

"I want to stand in the gap for you both. I want to support you in every way possible, and that includes financially. I want to help pay bills with you and help buy Christmas presents with you and help pay for Leo to go to college."

"What are you saying, Jackson?" she asked, starting to tear up.

"I'm saying that I want to live with you and Leo, wherever that may be. Here, there or yonder."

She smiled, suddenly a little upset that he wasn't asking for more. Her face must have shown her disappointment.

"What?" he said. She shook her head, trying to shake off the feeling.

"Nothing. Hey, do you want chicken or fish tonight?" She got up and started rummaging through the refrigerator that was now pulled into the middle of the small kitchen. Jackson pulled her hand away from the refrigerator door and turned her to face him.

"Don't lie to me, Rebecca," he said, more serious now. Her eyes started watering, betraying her confidence.

"I just thought... we were heading for more... than living together." She could barely get the words out, and she felt like such a sissy girl for saying that. She wasn't supposed to need a man, right?

"Oh my gosh, Rebecca!" he said, grinning from ear to ear as he pulled her into a tight hug. Her arms hung by her sides, confusion probably evident in her body language alone.

"Huh?" was all she managed to say when he finally let go and continued grinning in her face.

"You want more?" he said, his own eyes starting to water too. She felt confused and tilted her head as she looked at him, furrowing her eyebrows so hard that she was probably causing premature wrinkles.

"What?" Boy, she was quite the wordsmith today.

"I want more too, sweetie. I just didn't want to push you," he said softly as he leaned down and looked at her eye to eye. "I want it all. Do you understand me?"

She nodded slowly. "Yes…"

"But I want you to be really sure because I know this is hard for you. The memories…"

Of course, he was referring to the memories of her first marriage ending when her husband was killed in one of the World Trade Centers on September 11.

"I know you had planned on a long, happy marriage and that got taken from you. Honestly, I wasn't sure if you'd ever want to get married again, honey. That's why I asked about moving in together. Not because I don't want to make the ultimate commitment to you, Rebecca. I just wanted to respect the commitment you'd made before."

She was so touched that she started to weep, pressing her face into his chest. He wrapped his arms around her tightly and let her cry. He wasn't sure if she was crying out of sadness for what she'd lost all those years ago or crying because she was happy with him, but he just let her cry anyway. All of that could be worked out later.

RONNI WAITED for Brad to show up, anxious to surprise him. She'd texted him and told him to meet her at the theater knowing full well that he would complain about the location. After all, they worked there all day so the last place either of them wanted to be right now was at the Lamont.

But tonight she had something special planned, and the Lamont was the only place it could happen.

Brad finally appeared at the door wearing a pair of white cargo shorts and an aqua t-shirt. Against his tanned skin and dark hair, he looked sexier than any man she'd seen in California. Yep, those Southern boys just had something… special.

"Hey, good looking," she said as she slid her hands around his waist and planted a kiss on him.

"Well, hello…" he murmured through their kiss. "Wow."

She was stunning, wearing a tight royal blue dress that showed off all of her curves. Her high black heels accentuated her toned calves and newly tanned legs. She kept her blond hair down the way he liked it, straight and cascading over one shoulder.

"Come on. I have a surprise for you," she said, barely able to contain her excitement.

"This isn't the surprise?" he asked, teasing her as they walked and he pulled on the back of her dress. "Because I love this surprise…"

"I've been working on something this week," she said as she leaned against the door to the theater. Brad leaned in and kissed her neck.

"Well, I've been working on something for the last thirty seconds," he said, and she could feel what he'd been working on against her thigh.

"No, no, Brad Parker… Come on…" she said, pushing against the door with her hip. When they walked inside, Brad stopped in his tracks and his jaw dropped. Ronni stood there watching him, a huge grin finally overtaking his handsome face.

"What the… How did you find this?" he asked, pointing at the screen. There, in a still shot, was his favorite movie from his teenage years - "The Blue Alien" - a corny sci-fi flick that no one else liked and flopped majorly at the box office.

But for Brad, it was a masterpiece. He'd been talking about it for weeks, almost since the day they'd met. About how he'd seen it in theater B, and how his brothers had ribbed him for liking such a silly movie. About how he'd put his arm around Talia Booth and how she'd slid out from under it and changed seats.

Ronni smiled. "I had to make a lot of calls to find someone who didn't burn the reel," she said giggling. "I finally found a place in California who shipped it to me for a small fee."

"Ronni, I can't believe you did this for me. And we're going to watch it?" he asked, his mouth still hanging open.

"Of course. Look, I have dinner and dessert," she said, pointing to a table she'd set up in front of some seats in the middle where there was a wide enough walkway. She had a beautiful spread all set up with candles, chocolate dipped strawberries and even champagne.

He pulled her close to him. "You are my perfect woman," he said, but this time he didn't smile. He was totally serious.

"Ditto," she said.

"Wait. I'm your perfect woman?" Typical Brad.

"Shut up, and come on," she said as she pulled him toward the seats.

CHAPTER 10

*T*onight was the night that the family would gather together and wish Adele and Harrison well as they took off on their journey together. Brad couldn't help but feel conflicted because he'd soon be saying goodbye to Ronni too.

Maybe he should go with her. It was on his mind all the time, but tonight he wanted to focus on his mother.

"We're going to miss you," he said as he hugged her tightly.

It was the end of an era. Adele Parker had always been in January Cove. It was a comfort to know his mother was just around the corner if he needed her. Or if she needed him. But now, she had Harrison and that made everyone feel better about her leaving.

And then there was Tessa and Aaron. Madly in love and engaged. And Kyle and Jenna were enjoying married life and raising her daughter together. He expected a pregnancy announcement from those two any day now.

Jackson and Rebecca were making plans to rent the space above Jolt so they could move in together too.

Addison and Clay were raising a baby and running the B&B.

Yet again, Brad was feeling left out. The love of his life was leaving and going back to her life without him.

"You okay, son?" Adele asked, knowing when one of her kids was upset. There was no use in hiding it.

"Nothing to worry about, Mom."

"She's a keeper, Brad," Adele whispered into his ear. Ronni was across the room chatting with Jenna and Tessa, girly giggles rising above the conversation in the room.

"She's going home, Mom."

"Then change her mind."

"It's not that easy," he said. "I've tried."

"Well, not hard enough, apparently."

Leave it to Adele to get right to the point.

"Listen, honey, a woman needs to hear certain things."

"Such as?"

"I don't know. It's your job to figure that out," she said before Harrison grabbed her and pulled her away to speak to some guests who were arriving at her going away party.

Maybe his mother was right. He had to figure out just what to say to get Ronni to stay. He wasn't going to give up.

"I DON'T UNDERSTAND why you have to go to Atlanta," Brad said.

"One of the management team members is on a layover for twenty-four hours. He wants me to come up and go over our progress while he's here. I'll be back late tomorrow," Ronni said as she threw a few items in her overnight bag and Brad sat on the bed.

"I'll miss you," he said softly. She sat down beside him and kissed him on the cheek.

"Did I ever tell you how sweet you are?"

"No. I'd definitely remember that. You've told me

what a pain in the ass I am a few times, though." His dry humor always made her laugh.

"Well, you are sweet," she said, kissing him on the nose before she resumed packing. "And when I get back, I'll bring you a present."

"The only I present I need is you," he said, sweeping her down onto the bed and kissing her. And it was true. As far as Brad was concerned, she was all he ever needed.

THE LAMONT WASN'T the same without Ronni. Being alone in the old building used to bring back memories from childhood, but now all he could think about was her.

The conference room smelled like her perfume, and the doors to Theater B reminded him of their movie night. He still couldn't believe all the trouble she'd gone to.

Everything reminded him of her. The only consolation was that she'd be back in a few hours, so he tried his best to focus on the work at hand.

Even though they were head over heels for each other, they'd still managed to get a lot done in a short amount of time. The grounds were almost complete, with a mini golf course and a small carnival area being built from scratch. They planned to have a Halloween festival there in October, in fact.

Inside, there was new paint and flooring, and a brand new state-of-the-art arcade had been installed a week ago. Brad had to refrain from venturing off into the arcade or else he might not ever make it back out.

The theaters were getting an overhaul this week too. It was all coming together, and that made him even sadder. If Ronni went home, he wasn't sure what he would do.

"Excuse me?" a man said from behind him, startling him enough that he thought about using the stapler beside him as a weapon.

"Man, you scared the crap out of me. I thought the door was locked," Brad said as he stood up and puffed his chest out like some kind of wild bird trying to scare off a predator.

"Sorry," the guy said. He didn't look familiar, and he definitely didn't have a Southern accent. He looked every bit the part of "preppy" with an actual sweater tied around his neck. What was this? 1990?

"Can I help you?"

"I'm looking for Veronica Blair."

"Oh, you must be from California? Did you guys get your wires crossed? She's in Atlanta waiting for you..."

"I'm confused. She definitely didn't know I was coming. Took me awhile to find out where she was."

"Huh?" Brad was totally baffled. "Who are you again?"

"Evan Carlton," he said, reaching his hand out toward Brad. Evan. What on Earth was he doing there? Brad crossed his arms. "Did I do something to offend you?"

"Yeah. You left my friend at the altar. What kind of guy does that? Leaves a beautiful, smart, funny...."

"She left me."

One of the shortest sentences in history, but it took the wind out of Brad's sails. This guy had to be lying.

"What?"

"She left me," Evan said before letting out an ironic sounding laugh. "I guess she told you I left her? Wow. Unbelievable."

Brad leaned against the front counter, trying to take it all in. "So you're saying she left you? And I should believe that why?"

"I don't care if you believe it or not. Hell, I don't even know who you are!" Evan said. "Where is she?"

"None of your damn business," Brad said, seething for reasons he couldn't quite comprehend at the moment. Was he mad at this guy? Or was he mad at Ronni for lying?

"Listen, man, I don't know who you... Oh, wait. I get it now. She's with you, isn't she? Oh my God... She sure moved on fast. Wow." Evan shook his head and laughed. "I give up."

"You're telling the truth," Brad said, more to himself as a confirmation than anything else.

"Yes. I am. I came here to try to talk some sense into her, but I can see it's a lost cause. But at least I can save another man from her craziness."

"Don't talk about her like that," Brad warned.

"Fine. Protect her, but let me say what I need to say."

Brad nodded and walked into the conference room. Evan sat down across from him and leaned back in his chair.

"We were together for two years. Everyone thought we were perfect for each other. The business woman and the doctor. Wonderful life laid out before us. Planning kids and vacations. I let her plan the biggest wedding she wanted, all the bells and whistles from the Four Seasons Hotel to the top caterer in California. No expense was spared. The only thing she paid for was the caterer, and that was because she insisted on contributing. She always was a bit stubborn. Anyway… Then she bolted. Literally an hour before the wedding, she climbed out of the bathroom window just outside of the ballroom where almost two hundred guests waited. Thank God her maid of honor checked on her before I was left standing like a fool in front of our family and friends."

"And she didn't say anything?"

"Nope. Well, she texted me later, once she was long gone. It simply said 'I'm sorry'. I was worried sick. I finally bribed someone at her company to tell me where she was. They were very tight lipped, but I've found if you wave enough money in front of someone's face…"

"She must've had a reason," Brad said, trying to convince himself more than Evan.

"Does it really matter? Who does that to a person? Do you know how humiliating that was? And still I was willing to come here because I love her… and I know she still loves me. You can't fake that."

"Maybe she was."

"Well, maybe she is now too," Evan said. "Good luck, man. You're gonna need it."

And with that, he walked out and Brad was left wondering if it was all a big illusion.

BRAD SAT ON HIS SOFA, a beer in one hand and his cell phone in the other. He wasn't sure if he wanted to get a text from Ronni ever again, but if he did he didn't want to miss it.

His heart ached. A few short hours ago, he'd been longing for her and now he was wondering who she really was.

Evan was right. Who does that? Did she have a conscience? Was she just stringing him along too? Did she really care about him, or was she some kind of runaway bride character like in the movies?

Brad was startled out his thoughts by a knock at the door. When he opened it, he didn't expect to see her standing there.

"Surprise! My meeting ended early, so I drove straight here!" she said before kissing him on the lips. He didn't move. He didn't kiss her back. He just stood there, unable to make eye contact. "Brad? Is everything okay?"

"Yeah," he said as he stepped back to allow her

inside. He shut the door behind her and stood there, hands in his jean pockets.

"What's wrong?" she asked, clearly concerned by the look on her face. He honestly didn't know how to answer that, so he went with the simplest route.

"Evan."

Her face went pale. "What?"

"Evan came to see you today. Well, actually, Evan came looking for his runaway bride today." He walked around her and sat back down on the sofa before taking a long swig of his beer. It was empty within seconds. He crushed it and threw it across the room toward a trash can before popping open another one.

He wasn't a big drinker normally, but desperate times called for desperate measures. Right now, he just wanted to dull the pain of being lied to and strung along. At least that was how he saw it.

"Brad, let me explain…" she said as she crossed the room slowly.

"Explain? Seriously? What kind of explanation could you possibly have for spending so much money on a wedding and then climbing out a window an hour before? And then telling me that he left you standing at the altar? Are you some kind of compulsive liar?"

She took in a deep breath and wiped a tear that was already cascading down her cheek. The silence in the room was deafening. There was no explanation.

"I can't believe you lied to me, Ronni. I thought you really cared, but you were just playing me like you played Evan."

"That's not true! I didn't play you, Brad. I do care about you! I love you!" she said for the first time. Right now, it meant nothing. In fact, it caused him more pain. He shot up off the sofa.

"You don't love me! Stop telling me lies, Ronni! And why should I be surprised anyway? The only other woman I ever loved - who by the way I didn't love even a shred as much as I loved you - did the same thing to me that you did to Evan. I can't believe I fell for it again. At least I wasn't the idiot who spent all that money…"

She walked forward and grabbed his arms before he could bring another can up to his mouth and swiped it out of his hands and onto the floor where the contents started saturating the carpet.

"Now you listen to me, Brad Parker! You don't know the story, and maybe it won't matter, but you're going to sit down, shut up and listen to it.

Then, if you still don't want to be with me, I'll leave and never come back."

He breathed in and out of his nose, teeth clenched, like a bull about to charge, but he sat down and stared straight again. He couldn't look at her. She was too damn beautiful, and he was too damn angry.

"Fine. Talk." He leaned back on the sofa and stared at the ceiling as she began.

"I never loved Evan."

"Oh, that makes it all better."

"Are you going to let me talk or not?" His silence was her answer, so she continued. "Evan was a nice guy, or so I thought at the time. I was just making my way in business, and we met at a party." She stood up and walked around the room, pacing out of nervousness.

"I don't need the history of your dating life."

"Fine. I'll cut to the chase. He pushed very hard for marriage, and I went along with it when I shouldn't have. I knew from the start that he wasn't the man for me, but honestly all of my friends were settling down and I was starting to feel like my time would never come. He wooed me unlike any other man I'd dated."

"You mean he had money, and apparently you're a gold…"

"You finish that sentence, and I swear I'll slug you like a man!" she said, pointing her finger right in his face in an instant. "I'm not a gold digger, Brad. God, don't you know me at all?"

"Apparently not!" he yelled, finally looking at her. She looked exhausted, ragged almost. Not the beauty he knew, but someone who was digging deep into her soul for answers that would never be good enough for him.

"Listen," she said, sitting on the coffee table in front of him. "I was raised in a very bad situation. We never had anything. I always dreamed of a fairy princess wedding, so yes, I fell for all the stuff Evan could provide. The stability. I thought I could make the love happen at some point, but until then I'd be safe. The day of the wedding, I showed up totally planning to marry him. But I just couldn't do it, Brad. I didn't love him, and I felt sick. It wasn't nerves. I suddenly realized that it wasn't the life I wanted to lead. No amount of money is worth that… It felt like he wasn't my soul mate, and I believe in soul mates. I felt like I would be cheating on my soul mate, whoever he was. I can't explain it…"

Brad sat silently, unsure of what to believe anymore. He loved her, but he couldn't trust her.

"Why lie to me, Ronni? Why tell me that he abandoned you?"

"Because I was ashamed of myself, quite honestly. I should've talked to Evan and explained, but I just didn't have the courage at the time. I knew he would beg me to stay, and I couldn't do it. I was embarrassed, so I made something up. When I came to January Cove, it was an escape in so many ways. I never expected to fall in love. Real love," she said softly as she inched ever closer to him.

"I can't do this," he said.

"Can't do what?"

"This. This thing between us. I thought we had one kind of relationship, but we didn't. It was an illusion, Ronni."

"No, it wasn't," she pleaded as he stood up and walked across the room, his back facing her. "Everything else I said was totally real."

"Everything else?" he said with a laugh. "Except the important things, right? I mean, why be honest with the country bumpkin?"

"That's not fair, Brad," she said, standing and walking across the room. He wouldn't turn around.

"I think you should leave."

"So this is over between us? Just like that?" she asked softly. He didn't answer, so she picked up her purse and walked to the door. "Fine. But I have one thing to say. When I told you Evan left me at the altar, I lied. I get it. That was wrong. But I didn't know you very well at that time. I didn't know I would fall in love with you. I was just your boss, and I didn't want to talk about my personal life. I was going to tell you the truth, Brad. I just needed time."

He still didn't speak, mainly because he didn't know what to say. So she left quietly, and Brad was left standing in his living room worrying that he'd just made the biggest mistake of his life.

CHAPTER 11

*A*ddison put the final touches on the cake she'd baked for her new guests. A newly married couple had just checked in, and she was delighted to learn more about them and get them to try her new cake recipe.

"Yum. What's that?" Clay asked, reaching toward the thick white icing. She slapped his hand away.

"No, no… This is for the honeymooners…" she said with a smile. "I think I did pretty good."

"Let me taste it, and I'll tell you if it's good…"

"Clay Hampton, if you want to keep that hand, you'll move it right now!" she said playfully. He was like a big kid sometimes.

"Fine. Meanie," he said as he slumped down onto

the bar stool. "Hey, listen, I didn't know Ronni was leaving today, did you?"

"What? No. Brad didn't mention that. I wonder if he knows…"

"I was upstairs changing a light bulb in the bathroom, and I saw her packing her bag on her bed. When she ran into me in the hallway, she looked a bit stunned, actually, but she finally told me she was leaving. Some other guy is coming to take her place and finish the job. It was kind of weird."

"Uh oh. That doesn't sound good. I talked to Brad a couple of days ago and he was so head over heels about her. Something must've happened… Hey, can you deliver this cake to the couple while I go try to stop a disaster from happening?"

"Of course."

"And don't you dare eat any of that cake, Clay!" she chided as she removed her apron and folded it.

"Would I do a thing like that?"

"Yes."

"True," he said. "But, I won't. This time."

"Is she still upstairs?" Addy asked as she walked toward the foyer.

"No. She left about ten minutes ago. Not sure where she was going, but I know her flight doesn't leave until late tonight."

"I'm on it!" Addison called back as she ran out the front door.

BRAD SAT ON HIS SOFA, staring at some random show on TV. It was Saturday, the perfect day to sit around and lament the terrible turn his life had taken yet again.

Women. Can't live with them… Ah, he was too tired to even finish the thought.

Last night had been the worst night of sleep he'd gotten in years. Two hours. Two whole hours was all he got. He'd tossed, turned, popped a sleeping pill even, but nothing worked.

All he saw was Ronni in his mind.

No woman had ever turned him so upside down. He'd been a fool for believing in her. The only problem was, he didn't feel like a fool at the time. He felt whole and loved.

The sudden banging at his front door startled him out of his walking, or sitting rather, haze. He slowly, slothfully, made his way to the door, opening it to find Addison standing there with a frantic look on her face.

"What's wrong?" he asked, immediately springing

into "brother mode".

"She's leaving…" Addison said breathlessly, her quick paced walk from the B&B getting the better of her.

"Who's leaving?"

"Ronni. Tonight. Back to Cali…"

"Okay…" he said, pretending it didn't affect him, but inside his heart was beating wildly.

"Don't you care?" she asked as she pushed past him into the darkened living room. "Damn, Brad, did something die in here?" she asked, looking around at the empty pizza boxes and beer cans.

"Shut up," he said as he closed the door.

"You look like hell too," she said as she stared at her normally handsome brother. His hair was sticking up everywhere, his navy blue t-shirt stained with tomato sauce. He was wearing a pair of gray sweatpants with holes in them.

"Thanks. Can I help you with something?" he asked as he fell back onto the sofa. Addison couldn't believe her eyes. Her brother, the life of every party, was depressed.

"Um, I think I should be asking you that question. What on Earth happened between you and Ronni?"

"None of your business," he muttered. Without

warning, Addison leapt onto the sofa and put her hand around her brother's neck just like she had done so many times as a kid. She was strong for a petite woman.

"Cut it out, Addy!" he said in garbled speech as she squeezed.

"Listen up, buddy, you're going to tell me what happened or I'm going to give you a purple nurple and a wet willie and…"

"Fine," he whispered and she finally let go.

For the next few minutes, he recounted the whole thing. Ronni's initial story, Evan showing up, her confession… Addison took it all in without saying anything for a moment.

"You're an idiot," she finally said.

"Excuse me?"

"She's the perfect woman for you. You love her. She loves you. And you're sitting here like some kind of deranged redneck, holed up in your holey pants in the dark watching… what is that? A pie eating contest? Jeez…"

"She lied to me!"

"And?"

"So you'd be okay with Clay lying to you like that?"

"I lied to him, and everyone else, like that.

Remember?" she said softly. "And he forgave me, Brad. And look where we are now."

Brad was quiet. She was right. Her secret had been so much bigger than Ronni's, and Clay forgave her. They'd built an amazing life together already.

"Look, I know you've been burned before, and I'm sorry for that. But she made a mistake. She didn't know you well at the time. She didn't know if she could trust you either. So, she protected herself. I don't think she'd make the same choice again, Brad. Do you?"

"No. I don't. But how do I know that I can ever trust that she's telling me the truth?"

"Have you ever lied? Let he who is without sin cast the…"

"Addy, don't start quoting the Bible to me."

"But it's true. We've all lied! You can't just throw away this amazing woman that you so obviously love and not fight for her."

"I don't know. I need some time to think."

"Well, think fast, dear brother, because her flight leaves soon and she's going to be driving to the airport. In fact, I don't know where she is right now."

BRAD SPENT two hours driving all over January Cove looking for Ronni's car, but he couldn't find it. She was gone. She had to be. Her room at the B&B was cleaned out, and none of the Parker siblings or their partners had seen her.

In an effort not to drive himself crazy, he drove to the Lamont. He needed something to distract him. As he drove up, he was shocked to see her car sitting there, parked behind the dumpster.

At first, he was worried something had happened to her, so he ran to the car but she wasn't inside. The only other place she could be was inside the building, so he keyed the side door and walked into the lobby.

She wasn't in the lobby and she wasn't in the conference room. He was starting to get a little worried, to be honest, so he checked Theater A but she wasn't there either.

Next, he ran quickly around the building looking for her. Very little crime ever happened in January Cove, but there was a first for everything.

His heart rate picked up as he ran outside and looked around the mini golf course and the new go-cart ramps that were being built. Where was she?

The only place he hadn't checked yet was Theater B, so he ran through the lobby once again and pulled the door open. And there she was. Thank God, he thought, as he took a deep breath.

He wasn't prepared for what he saw. She was sitting in one of the seats watching "The Blue Alien". He walked slowly around to the side and noticed she was crying. Her face was stained with tears as she wiped her eyes with a tissue.

"Ronni?" he said just loud enough for her to hear him over the movie. She didn't have the sound turned up very loud at all, but he still had to raise his voice. It startled her and she jumped up, thankful to see it was Brad but then a look of sadness mixed with anger took over her face.

"What are you doing here?" she asked, more rhetorically than anything, before sitting down again and staring blankly at the screen.

"You liked this movie enough to watch it again?" Brad asked with a smile. The smile was wasted, though, because she wasn't looking in his direction at all.

"No. Actually, I think it's the dumbest movie I've ever seen."

Brad walked closer. "Then why are you watching it?"

"None of your damn business," she said before she stood up and walked toward the lobby quickly.

He had to run to catch up, but he finally caught her in the conference room.

"Ronni, why were you watching that movie?" he pressed.

"Why does it matter, Brad?" she asked, tears pouring from her eyes. "You hate me, or at least you don't love me anymore, so why are you so worried about what movies I watch?" She blew her nose into the tissue and threw it in the trashcan before grabbing another one out of the box she had nestled under her arm.

"I'm so sorry, Ronni," he said softly as he put his hand on her shoulder. She didn't move.

"Sorry for what?" she asked, sounding like she had a bowling ball stuffed in her nose.

"For being a first class jackass."

She slowly turned around to face him, her nose red from blowing it and her eyes red from crying. "I'm listening..."

"Sit down," he said, leading her to the chair. He sat in another chair and pulled it in front of her, his knees touching hers. "I've been a fool, and I'm so sorry. My sister set me straight."

"She did?"

"I'm not perfect. You're not perfect. But you didn't set out to hurt me, and I know that now. Can I have another chance?" he asked as he reached for her hand.

"Even if I wanted to give you another chance, I'm leaving tonight. I'm going home, Brad."

"I know that's the plan, but you don't have to go home. Stay here with me. We have something special, Ronni."

"I'm sorry, Brad. I do love you, but I have to go home. My life is there."

The air felt like it had just been sucked from his lungs. He'd apologized and professed his love yet again, but she was still leaving.

"I don't understand. Why are you still leaving?" he asked, standing up and pacing the room like the Parker man that he was.

"I have a job and an apartment and a dog at my friend's house."

"So get a new job and an apartment here, and I'll buy you a big bag of dog food."

"Brad, be serious."

"I am being serious."

"I can't stay here. The opportunities are so limited with my career…"

"Then I'll come with you," he said. She stood up and held his hands in hers.

"I've enjoyed getting to know you, and I can't

believe how fast I fell in love with you. But this wasn't going to work from the start. I'm a West coast kind of girl, and you're a Southern gentleman with sea water running through his veins. I'll always love you, Brad Parker, but this is where our story ends."

A knife through his heart would've felt better right now.

"Goodbye, Brad," she said softly into his ear before kissing his cheek. "Thank you for loving me."

And with that, Ronni Blair walked out of the conference room, out of the Lamont and straight out of his life.

TWO WEEKS HAS PASSED, and Brad still wasn't used to working with the new guy that the Drake Corporation had sent to take Ronni's place. His name was Dave, and his picture was right next to the word "nerd" in the dictionary.

He hadn't heard a word from Ronni since she left. Not a text or a phone call or an email. Nothing.

He'd screwed up the courage to ask Dave about her one time, but all he got in return was that she'd made it back to California and was busy with a new project.

The Lamont project was in its final stages and would open in just about three weeks. The public was getting excited, and plans were being made for more tourist attractions in January Cove in the future.

But today was a day off from work as Brad and the family gathered for family dinner at the house that now belonged to Aaron. He and Tessa were still happily planning their October wedding in a few weeks.

"So, this is my dress," Tessa said, holding a magazine close to her chest as she showed Jenna. "Don't you dare look, Aaron Parker!" she chided as Aaron playfully pretended that he was trying to look.

"Oh, it's gorgeous, Tessa," Jenna cooed.

They were all full of food and stories as they sat on the screened porch. It was weird not to have Adele there, but she'd been traveling for a couple of weeks now and was checking in via text regularly. Right now they were in Maine, and she was as happy as they'd ever seen her.

"Hey, let's get Mom on Skype for a minute," Kyle said to Jenna. She smiled and nodded.

"Why are we getting Mom on Skype?" Brad asked.

"Well, don't you miss her?" Jenna asked, poking

him in the side. Yes, he missed his mother, but the woman he really missed was on the other coast.

After a few failed attempts, Adele appeared on the iPad. Everyone said hello, and she looked so well rested and happy. Content was a good word for it. They could see the ocean in the background and Harrison was sitting right beside her.

"Hey, Mom! Do you miss us?" Kyle asked.

"Of course, my sweeties!"

"How's the trip going?" Aaron asked.

"Oh, wonderful. We've had such a good time. We stopped in Colonial Williamsburg a few days ago. And today we're hanging here on the beach, drinking margaritas and eating ham sandwiches."

"Sounds like a celebrity lifestyle you got there, Mom," Jackson said with a laugh. "Margaritas and ham sandwiches..." he whispered to Rebecca.

"Well, Mom, Jenna and I wanted to call you because we actually have an announcement to make to the whole family."

"How exciting! What is it, dear?" Adele said, inching closer to the screen.

"We're pregnant!" Jenna squealed like she was about to burst.

The room erupted in laughter and more squeals,

from the women mainly, and Adele grinned from the other side of the screen.

"I'm so excited for you both. I can't wait to meet him or her!"

"Thanks, Mom. We'll let you get back to your drunken ham sandwich party," Kyle said. Adele shook her finger at the screen.

"Kyle Parker..."

"Yes, Mom. I'm sorry..." he said before he ended the call.

"Congratulations, guys. I'm so happy for you," Brad said smiling. He was happy for them, but he was also sad for himself. Everyone was moving forward, and his life seemed to being moving backward.

As they all talked and planned, Brad slipped outside into the garden. He felt close to his mother there, looking at all of her roses and herbs still growing as if she was here. But even she was living her dream, and he seemed stuck on start.

"Hey, brother," he heard Addison say from behind him. She held his precious little niece, Anna Grace, in her arms. She was getting so big. How did time pass so quickly the older he got? Except for the last two weeks. Those passed like he was walking through quicksand.

"Hey," he said. He pulled a stray dead leaf off one of the shrubs and tossed it into the grass.

"You okay?"

"Nope." Honesty was the best policy, right?

"I figured. Have you heard from her?"

"Nope."

"Want to be alone?" she asked.

"Yep," he said. He smiled at her, and she just hugged him quietly for a moment before turning back to the house.

So many times in his life, he'd been at a fork in the road, but this time he had no power over which path to take. She didn't want to stay, and she didn't want him to come with her. He had no choice but to get over her.

But he couldn't imagine ever being able to do that.

CHAPTER 12

*R*ebecca stood in the kitchen of her new rental home. The little aqua blue beach house was across the street from Jolt, allowing her to keep an eye on her business day and night. She literally had a thirty foot commute to work.

"Last box!" Jackson yelled as he walked through the front door from across the street. No moving vans were needed for this move. Leo would be back from his mission trip later today, and he would be so surprised that they had moved across the street.

She knew he'd love the place. He got his very own room and a deck overlooking the water. What more could a teenage boy need?

"I'm exhausted," Rebecca said as she fell onto the sofa.

"Well, it's done, and now I get to live everyday with the prettiest girl on the planet," he said as he slid down beside her.

"Are you glad we did this?" she asked, leaning her head into the side of his chest.

"Absolutely. You?"

"I'm thrilled."

"So do you give me permission to one day ask you to marry me, Rebecca?" he asked, surprising her. She sat up and squinted her eyes at him.

"Are you asking me?"

"No. We just moved. Too much for one day," he said laughing.

"True."

"I just want permission to ask. One day."

"You have my permission," she said as she slid back down.

"Good."

BRAD DROVE up to the ferry landing after getting a call from Clay. It had now been five weeks since Ronni left, and it hadn't gotten any easier. The Lamont project was done and set to open in a few days, but he could barely drive past it now. Sheer determination and the need for his paycheck were the only things that got him through the rest of the job.

"Hey, man. What's up?" Brad asked when he saw Clay.

"I need some help."

"With?"

"We had a wedding on the island last night, but it was so late I had to leave all the rental chairs there. Mind riding over with me and helping me load them up?"

It was a weird request since he'd never known Clay to just leave rental chairs on the island like that, but he had a new baby he probably wanted to get home to.

"Sure."

Clay started the ferry, and they began the short drive over.

"So, how are you doing, dude? Haven't seen you around much lately."

"I'm hanging in there, I guess," Brad said as he opened a soda and leaned against the railing.

"Heard from Ronni?"

"No. And I wish everyone would quit asking me that."

"Sorry," Clay said, a hint of a smirk on his face. Brad kind of wanted to punch him.

They rode in silence for the rest of the way, but when Clay pulled up, Brad didn't see any chairs.

"Where are the chairs?"

"Oh, we had the wedding on the other side," Clay said as he roped off the ferry.

"Huh? On the rocky side?"

"Yeah. Weird, I know. But the couple apparently had a special moment over there so we did what they asked." Clay started walking toward the beach while Brad followed behind him still confused about the location of the chairs.

When they crossed through the trees and to the rocky side of the beach, there were still no chairs.

"Dude, where are the chairs? I've got stuff to do."

"Oh, dang it. I must have loaded them last night and forgot," Clay said, now not making eye contact and hurriedly heading toward the ferry.

"Where are you going?" Brad called, trying to keep up.

"Help! Help!" a female voice called from the left side of where he was. Given the choice of following Clay or helping a damsel in distress, Brad ran toward the damsel's voice.

It was a familiar voice, now that he thought about it.

"Did someone call for help?" he said loudly as he walked to the edge of the wooded area.

"Up here!" the voice said.

Ronni.

Sitting in a tree.

Sitting in THEIR tree.

"Ronni?" he breathed out, both excited and relieved to see her and confused at her being in a tree. In January Cove. And not in California.

"Hey, Brad," she said with a big grin on her face. "Wanna help me down from here?"

"Last time I tried that, you got hurt."

"Well, in fairness, I did jump."

He walked to the bottom of the tree and reached up as she gingerly slid down into his arms. His waiting, aching, lonely arms.

She felt perfect in his arms. She fit against him like she was made for him, and he didn't even realize how much he missed her until he could feel her heart beating against his chest again.

For a moment, he just held her, smelling her hair and feeling the warmth of her against him. Realizing she was probably just there for the grand opening, he let her go and stepped back.

"How are you?" he said.

"Good. How are you?"

He wanted to say "good" but he didn't want to lie. "Horrible."

"What's wrong?" she asked, stepping forward to close the gap between them.

"Well, you see, there was this woman. This amazing, beautiful, smart, funny woman. She was totally perfect for me. We had an argument, but we made up. But then she chose a different life that didn't have me in it. And I miss her. And I love her."

There it was. The most vulnerable moment in his life.

"Wow. That's a sad story. How does it end?"

"She left."

"That's not how I heard the ending of that story. I heard that she went home, figured out that it wasn't her home anymore because he wasn't there, packed her stuff, loaded up her dog and all of her worldly possessions and drove all the way to January Cove to her new rental apartment above a place called Jolt."

Brad's heart literally skipped a beat. His eyes met hers, and she was smiling. She looked happy and relaxed and at home.

"What?"

Ronni stepped forward, careful not to trip on the

rocks and ruin the moment, and put her hands on his upper arms.

"Brad Parker, I love you. I tried to go back to my life, but it wasn't my life anymore. I just had to make sure. So, I talked to my boss and he agreed to relocate me here. I'll be running day-to-day operations of the Lamont and overseeing new tourist attractions along the coast."

"Are you serious?" he said, struggling not to cry. He was a man's man, after all.

"Totally serious. So, I'm here for good. I'd love to be your girlfriend... if you'll have me," she said softly.

"I'd have you right here if I didn't know Clay was standing right over there!" he called out.

"Gross," Clay called back. "I'll come back later!"

"Way later," Brad called before he turned his attention and his lips to the love of his life.

CHECK out Rachel's other books at www. RachelHannaAuthor.com.